ASTEROIDS!

STORIES OF SPACE ADVENTURE

T.E. ACKERSON   JOSEPH BENEDETTO
MISHA BURNETT   RON N. BUTLER
KENNETH B. CHIACCHIA   ROY GRAY
GEOFFREY HART   BRUCE F. WEBSTER

Edited by
OREN LITWIN

LAGRANGE
BOOKS

Published by Lagrange Books, an imprint of Oren Litwin
Visit our website at https://lagrangebooks.com
Contact us at editor@lagrangebooks.com.

The stories within this volume are works of fiction. Any resemblance to any person, alive or dead, is unintentional.

Cover by Deranged Doctor Design: http://www.derangeddoctordesign.com

STORIES OF SPACE ADVENTURE

ASTEROIDS!

TIM ACKERSON • J. F. BENEDETTO
MISHA BURNETT • RON N. BUTLER
KENNETH B. CHIACCHIA • ROY GRAY
GEOFFREY HART • BRUCE F. WEBSTER
EDITED BY OREN LITWIN

CONTENTS

INTRODUCTION

OREN LITWIN

When I was young, I encountered W.H. Auden's stark poem "In Praise of Limestone," and was powerfully affected by it. In part, Auden describes how the encounter with "immoderate soils" makes a mockery of our social niceties and strips life down to its essence. "I am the solitude that asks and promises nothing; / That is how I shall set you free."

Asteroids, to me, capture something of that encounter. Shattered fragments of stardust, ungentled by the wind and waves and workings of life, asteroids are and always will be a place where humanity is not welcome. Too small to have much gravity or air to breathe, floating aimlessly through the blackness of space, capable of immense destruction if one should cross the path of an inhabited planet—asteroids seem to promise only the coldness of death.

And yet, that very promise has an attraction. Humanity measures itself against the challenges we overcome. We seek out harsh conditions to test our mettle; and what harsher than an asteroid? In a sense, asteroids will forever be the last frontier, beckoning to those who seek not material comfort but achievement.

The stories in this volume, though they vary greatly in tone, each capture something of our drive to measure ourselves against the stark existence that an asteroid offers. Some asteroids contain valuable metals which can make their finders rich—or provide the motive for murder, in J.F. Benedetto's "The Dead Men on Asteroid 3-19 Delta." Other asteroids, like the one in T.E. Ackerson's "Fabio-14 (ETC.)," are just a place to work a farm and make a living, which gets trickier when you have alien neighbors. And sometimes an asteroid is a place to be safe, away from other people, in Misha Burnett's "Fragile."

Geoffrey Hart's "The Shot Launched Around the World" features an out-of-this-world advertising stunt, and a cameraman who has his own angle. Crevices in ancient rock are full of stark truths and lurking dangers, in Kenneth B. Chiacchia's "Resonance." And Space Marshal Rory Rammer must deal with a space miner with an inordinate fondness for nuclear explosions, in Ron N. Butler's "The Planetoid of Doom."

Roy Gray presents a tale of ecological catastrophe and interdimensional paradox, in "Rumblings." And Bruce F. Webster revisits the "SunDog" universe to tell of a desperate attempt to escape a world-killing asteroid—and make a profit in the process —in "Bad Egg."

The production of this book was funded by our fantastic backers on Kickstarter, and we owe them a great deal of thanks. It is an act of faith to give your support to a book that no one has read—rather like lifting off in a rocket to an unexplored region of space. I can only hope that our backers' faith has been rewarded. We are deeply grateful to our backers:

Joseph Benedetto, our "Patron of the Arts";

Sam Asher, Christine Gourley, Ron Laliberte, and Heidi Pilewski, our "Explorers of Worlds";

Ron Butler and Betty P. Thomas, our "Cosmic Cartographers";

Dagmar Baumann, Chris January, Chris Nash, Matthew Urick, and an anonymous backer, our "Astro-Archivists";

Mark Carter, Fred Herman, and Travis Siegel, our "Data-Dump Managers"; and

"Jim Henderson (author of the Mantis Saga)," "Raymond Solar," Kiong (Andy) Yeoh, and an anonymous backer, our "Space Cadets."

With that, I'll leave you to it. Ignition in five, four, three, two...

THE DEAD MEN ON ASTEROID 3-19 DELTA

JOSEPH BENEDETTO

OF ALL THE things I thought might happen on my first day as a security inspector at Mining Station 3, having an entire dig team die certainly wasn't one of them. But they did, an hour after I arrived on station. An airlock opened of its own accord and killed five miners.

Five men, one-third of the station's complement, dead.

And it fell to me to find out why.

I'm not a "security inspector" by training, you understand. I am… okay, *was*… a "blue-coat," a police detective in Draper City on Mars. But then the "glorious revolution" came and with it, certain changes. The kind that labeled me "politically unreliable" because I did not show "the proper revolutionary spirit" for a member of the "New" Martian Police Force. So, to get me out of everyone's hair, I was assigned (read: exiled) to corporate overwatch duty in the Asteroid Belt.

There are six companies that mine the Belt; luck of the draw got me liaised to Ling Standard Metals. Of course, the people at Ling Standard were none too happy with this—after all, no one likes having a cop looking over their shoulder all day. So, to get me out of everyone's hair, I was assigned (read: exiled) to Security Inspection of the Mining Circuit.

That's one benefit of running a business a hundred million miles from home: you can make up job titles, assign them to people you don't want around, then send them off on make-work tasks.

There are over 200 asteroids larger than 50 miles in diameter, and about a million more that have a diameter of half-a-mile or more, and any one of those can have a mining station. So to get rid of me, they made me a "security inspector" for the Ling Standard stations scattered across their section of the Belt... and sent me out here.

Mind you, when they came up with my make-work "job," I'm pretty sure that no one expected five miners would die in a freak airlock accident less than one hour after I arrived. Now, I know that working in the Belt entails a lot of risk, and I believe in coincidence and all that, but five men, all at the same time, in the kind of accident the engineers say is physically impossible? No. In my book, that's not a coincidence.

That's murder.

I'd shuttle-hopped out to MS-3 with two other people: Gregor Kaminski, a geologist-auditor for Ling Standard that Mining Station 3 had asked for, and Yu Chen, some Ling Standard VIP's niece coming along to see how things worked in a real mining station. Kaminski was the quiet type and didn't talk much; Yu, on the other hand, loved to talk. By the time we reached Mining Station 3, currently bolted to Asteroid 19 in Section Delta, I knew almost nothing about Kaminski, but I could fill a book about Yu, her parents (Heng and Cai), her boyfriend (Alan), her home (Level 5-under of Dome Epsilon in Opportunity City) and her career goals (an upper-management job in Ling Standard Metals).

I know it sounds callous, but after being locked up in a

10'x15' shuttle compartment all the way to MS-3 with this chatterbox, I almost welcomed it when the alarms sounded.

The details of what happened were simple enough. Mining Station 3 is shaped roughly like a "T" that docks itself, standing up, to the surface of a suitable asteroid and latches on with bore hooks to the surface, since the asteroids have no gravity to speak of. The shuttle dock is on top of the T and the living quarters and main offices are located in the opposite arms of the T; the vertical shaft that runs down to the surface contained the work labs, an open circulation space lined with conduits and power couplings and balconies, and, at the very bottom, the crew airlock leading out to the surface of the asteroid itself.

The five men who died, Dig Team One, were at the bottom of the T getting ready to head out to the surface. They had done the usual 30-minutes of pre-breathing 100% O2 to purge their bodies of nitrogen—the mining station air is 72% oxygen, 28% nitrogen at 5 psi, which provides an atmospheric mix similar to Terran sea level, albeit with a third of the air pressure. After purging their bodies of nitrogen gas they started putting on their space suits, a task that takes maybe 45 minutes.

They never finished. The airlock outer door opened itself to vacuum, and all five miners and their gear were blown out.

None of them had their suit helmets on yet. Death was not pretty, but at least it was quick.

The shuttle that had brought me, Kaminski and Yu to MS-3 undocked and went after the bodies while the remaining station personnel—Dig Team Two and the Senior staff—worked to get the airlock sealed again. I stayed the hell out of the way.

They had no trouble closing the airlock. Both the inner and outer doors responded to remote control just fine, which was bad; if one or the other had balked, the problem might have been obvious. But they didn't, which gave no hint as to why the airlock had opened itself.

And since I was Ling Standard's "security inspector" on-site —for what that make-work title was worth—I decided to find out what the hell happened.

I began by questioning everyone, starting with the two people who arrived with me, in order to get an outsider's view of the accident. I met with Kaminski in an unused room off the Mess Hall.

The lean redheaded scientist was the kind of lab-rat who was married to his test equipment. "I was in the GeoLab, looking over the ore samples that the dig teams had brought in, when I heard someone shouting," Kaminski told me, his face pale. "I went out onto the balcony... it opens into the circulation space above the airlock level... and I looked over to see what was going on. It was one of the miners. He yelled up to me, said that they were having a problem with the airlock. I asked him what was wrong and he shouted back that there was some kind of fault with the indicators, that the main door was—well, I didn't hear the rest; that's when the airlock blew out."

The small pale blue room we floated in felt even smaller as we talked about the fate of five dead men; it even smelled like death, although I hoped that was just my imagination. The after-effects of the explosive decompression and all that. "Did you note the time?" I asked.

He rubbed the back of his neck. "Well, no... there was a rush of air straight down the circulation space, so I knew the airlock had blown out. I mean, I'm only human! I kicked off the balcony rail and pushed myself back into the lab so that I would be behind the pressure door when it closed!"

I didn't disagree with his choices. The circulation space was a wide-open white shaft above the airlock level; it not only allowed the miners enough room to move large items between the airlock level and the labs above, but also provided an open, multi-level space that could be used for zero-g tumbles and exercise by the staff. It was *supposed* to be closed off above the suit room level by a special air-tight barrier; but the barrier had been removed over a year earlier by a previous work crew in order to speed up moving ore samples from the airlock level up to the labs.

Then again, there was no reason *not* to remove it; after all, it's impossible for an airlock to fail, right? *Right.*

When the airlock failed, the pressure doors at each level above the airlock would close automatically once the air pressure fell far enough. If Kaminski had remained on the balcony to see what was happening, he would have been trapped and died out there. "And you stayed in the GeoLab until they came and got you out, is that it?"

"Yes." He worriedly scratched at his right hand. "I... I tried! I mean, I checked to make sure the lab was sealed off, but after that... I just didn't know what to do—I'm just a geologist-auditor! I've never even been out of the headquarters lab until this trip! Oh sure, I took the standard civil-defense course in explosive decompression back in high school on Mars, but—"

"Yeah." I used my stylus to scribble another note on my holo-comp. He looked like he was going to puke, never a good thing in zero-g. I pulled a vomit bag from the wall dispenser and handed it to him. "That's it for now. Send in Yu, will you?"

I pegged Yu as being of Northern Chinese blood, based on her stockier build, lighter skin and thinner eyes. Her black ponytail floated weirdly behind her, though, and if I thought Yu was talk-ative before, I was wrong; once she truly got going, I couldn't shut her up. She bounced—literally, in zero-g—from one powder-blue plastic surface of the room to the next, changing orientation at will, facing me right-side-up one moment and then upside-down the next, all the while keeping up a one-sided dialogue. "I heard about such things but I never thought I'd be there when it happened. It happens on Mars, but only in the outside work camps. There hasn't ever been an airlock failure in Opportunity City. Do you think it's a mechanical fault in the door design? They'll have to redesign all the doors if it is. Do you know how many doors that would entail? It—"

"Yu!" I said, halting her verbal diarrhea. "Where were you when it happened?"

She blinked, as if she had never expected the question. "Main offices in the west wing. Top of the T and turn left. I had an appointment with the Station Director. Did you know that the term 'west wing' is Old Terran? It was a NorthAm label for the sector of a building where the main offices are. We sure use a lot of NorthAm terms on Mars. In fact, Common Language has more terms in NorthAm than it does in RusFed or Chinese. I bet that's because the NorthAm Union used to—"

"Yu!" She stopped talking, and I took a welcome breath of the silence. "Did you see anyone acting strangely? Notice anything unusual?"

She paused. "Well, once the pressure-drop alarm sounded, everyone—"

"*Before* the alarm," I said, wiping my hand down my face.

"Oh." She cocked her head in thought. "It's probably not important, but the overhead lights, the ones in the hallway leading into the main offices? They flickered right before the decompression alarm sounded. Do you think it has something to do with what happened? It might be indicative of an electro-mechanical failure. Do you think it could have been an electro-mechanical failure? That would explain the flickering lights. But airlocks are designed so that it's impossible for both doors to be open to vacuum at the same time. It's not supposed to happen. Well, they *say* it's not supposed to happen. But—"

"*Thank you!*" I said a little too loudly, pulling my holocomp close. I thought being in this little blue room with Kaminski had made it feel small; with Yu it became positively claustrophobic. "Could you go find the Station Director and send her in?"

Station Director Gonella was cool to me, although I figured it as the boss cloaking herself to cover her own ass, in case whatever had happened was somehow traced back to her. She clipped herself off to a nearby handhold, folded her arms in across her black jumpsuit and just floated in zero-gravity by the wall, one untamed curl of blonde hair drifting out above her forehead. "All I do know is what Dig Team One said: that once the GeoAud got here, they'd all be going home."

I looked up from my holocomp. "Home? Why?"

She gave a nonchalant half-shrug. "None of them would say. They'd just smile every time we asked. They *must* have made a strike. But whatever it was that they found, they wouldn't tell anyone what it was."

I frowned. "Aren't they required to report their findings?"

Gonella gave a rude grimace. "Yes! But they didn't. Didn't want to share whatever it was with the rest of us." She must have noticed my confused scowl. "Any dig team that locates a truly major find is eligible for 5% of the sales price of the refined ore," she explained. "It's bonuses like that which keep people out here so far from home; every dig team hopes to hit something valuable, something big enough to put them back on Mars or even Terra worry-free for the rest of their life."

Well, it was a motive, and one of the best; money is always an excellent reason to kill someone for, let alone five someones. "So you think they had made a strike, then? What kind? What would it have to be to make them rich?"

She waved her hand in irritation, sending her drifting out to the length of her tether. "Who knows? The metallic asteroids we're mining are about 80% iron; the rest are a mixture of nickel, iridium, platinum, gold and other precious metals, like osmium and rhodium."

"Don't you scan each asteroid before you choose one to lock onto for mining?"

"Yes," Gonella said, "but the sensor array we use can't be sure 100% of the time. Sometimes it's *way* off. That's why if we get a hunch on a rock, we'll dock to it, get out and do core drilling on the surface, get samples of everything and check them out. Maybe one time in five or six we have to send the samples back to LS Central Control to get them analyzed. That's what the GeoAud back at LSCC does. But for a dig team to ask that a GeoAud be sent out to do the analysis on-site? It'd have to be something really rare. They must not have been certain of their finding—or maybe they just wanted the GeoAud to verify the size of their strike. In either case, they would have been in line for a percentage payment *and* rotation back home if they turned up a truly rare find."

"Like a vein of solid gold?"

She pushed her shoulders back. "Possibly. Right now a ton of gold is worth $40,000,000. A 5% bonus on that would result in $2,000,000 for the dig team that found it—and that's for *each* ton of gold eventually mined out. Or rhodium. It's going for twice what gold goes for on the European Market right now. Imagine what hitting a multi-ton vein of *that* would mean for the dig team that found it. For that kind of money, I'd be secretive as well."

It was certainly a motive for murder. "What about the team that *didn't* find it? What would they get?"

"Absolutely nothing," Gonella admitted. "That's one reason why we restrict the dig teams to opposite sides of an asteroid, to keep one team from claim-jumping any finds made by the other team."

That made sense. "So the other dig team couldn't 'find' the claim and pretend it was their own?"

"No … there's no way they could officially be in Dig Team One's area."

"Not even if the GeoAud finds something spectacular in the ore samples that Team One brought in?"

Gonella's mouth pursed into a frown. "No. If the GeoAud turns up solid gold, the company'll arrange for a mining unit to come straight out. We just do the surveying and preliminary work; the actual extraction is done by a different arm of the company."

"So if it is a valuable strike, then Dig Team Two gets nothing?"

"Not a penny."

I looked aside, momentarily rebuffed. I had figured someone on Team Two had seen that Team One was about to get rich, and decided to eliminate them and take their claim. But if there was no way for anyone on Team Two to benefit from the murders, then why carry them out at all?

The wall console chimed, and Gonella stretched out and activated it. "Station Chief."

The speaker clicked on. It was Kaminski. "Uh, yes, Ms. Gonella? This is the GeoAud. I thought you should know. I just finished checking all of the ore samples that DG-1 brought in. I'm afraid that virtually all of the samples are an iron sulfide with the chemical formula $FeS2$."

Gonella's face curdled. "Pyrite?"

"That is correct."

"Impossible! They weren't stupid enough to mistake pyrite for gold!"

Kaminski's voice on the comm was fairly sure of itself. "Well, there *are* significant traces of both actual gold and arsenic occurring as a coupled substitution in the pyrite structure of many of the samples … but my tests show that overall, it's no more than 1.31% gold by weight. It might have been enough to confuse the

sensors, at least initially. I assume that's why they called for me …
to sort it all out one way or the other."

Gonella sighed. "That's why they asked for the GeoAud to
come out, then. To verify what it was they found."

"Yeah," I said, pulling at my chin. They thought they had the
real thing, a huge strike. They called for a geologist-auditor to
come out and verify it. Which caused someone—singular or
plural—to kill them. But who?

I realized Gonella was staring at me, waiting. "So," I asked,
"what happens next? To the station, I mean?"

Gonella studied her hands, which looked red for some reason.
"Ling Standard will shut us down and pull us back to CC for re-
outfitting."

"And this asteroid?"

"Given the fact there's nothing here and five men died on it,
rock 19-Delta will be written off."

"What about the other mining companies in the Belt? Would
any of them try to mine it?"

"It's in *our* section," she pointed out. "One of the other
companies might try to sneak in and mine it, but so what? Who
needs pyrite that badly?"

I blew out a breath, which caused me to drift backward from
where I had been floating and fumble for the nearest handhold
on the blue plastic wall. Once I had recovered my dignity, I said,
"I'd like to interview the rest of the station staff."

It didn't go as I expected. Of the five senior staff who ran the
station, each of them had an alibi for the time preceding the
accident: a three-hour meeting that no one left. The one who was
the most voluble was also the most helpful: Engineer Walter
Potemkin. He had a stubborn face and the broad build of a
groundside engineer; it turned out that, like me, he was a

Martian who had been classified "politically unreliable," although his exile to the Belt had involved a much more voluntary departure than mine had.

"If you were to ask me," he said, as if I had not just asked him, "I'd say it was done by someone using a JC-console. Here, let me show you." He glided across the meeting room to a control panel on the wall sealed over with a transpex cover. Bracing himself, he lifted the cover free and let it drift off in zero-g, then pulled the unit clear of the wall via two hand-holds sticking up from either side of the console. He indicated back over his shoulder. "See that panel on the far wall, the yellow one with the black edging? There are panels like that in half of the compartments on the station."

He kicked off over to the yellow panel, braced himself again, and pulled the panel up. Inside were nothing but cable runs; no controls, no switches, no comp screens. He took hold of the control unit. "The Jump-Circuit console fits into these openings like this." He shoved it into place with an audible *click*. "The unit allows personnel who are out-of-position to execute damage control by temporarily linking into the control circuitry via induction clamps on the cable array. In addition to getting readouts of all the station sensors, it can be used to issue remote commands."

"Like, say, opening an airlock remotely?"

He gave a nod. "That's one of the easiest things to do. Remember, these things are designed for emergency damage control; the commands to open and close the airlock doors are right at the top of the list."

I floated myself over and looked at it, fighting to get my feet to the same plane Potemkin had *his* feet in. "Out of curiosity, what happens in the main offices when you put this thing on the cables?"

He gave a minute shrug, a tiny movement that was enough to

show emotion without making him start to drift away in zero-g. "Nothing shows."

"Would using it make the lights flicker?"

Potemkin frowned, then shook his head. "It shouldn't, but the way these station-ships are maintained... shoddy repairs, back splicing, short-cutting a wiring run to save repair time... it could. But I doubt it. I mean, this circuit isn't under any kind of load."

"But they might flicker, if the circuit it was attached to *was* under a large load?"

He pulled it free from the wall and closed the access panel. "Yeah, it might."

It looked like the five Senior Staff were not suspects, given their alibis. That left me with the five members of Dig Team Two, who had been my main suspects to begin with. The fact that Team One had only found pyrite was irrelevant; up until Kaminski's analysis of the ore samples, everyone on the station had suspected Team One of having made a rich strike. So, someone on Team Two was the most likely suspect. Only I ran into a major problem: all five miners on Team Two had alibis, just as good as the ones for the Senior Staff. All five were at dinner together, and they had been paged by the Senior Staff who were in their meeting, and so the two groups had seen each other via the wallscreen. Which meant that each group could verify where the other was at the time of the incident.

I floated myself across the empty blue room, staring at the stowed JC-console. Either it really had been just a freak accident, in which case everyone on the station was innocent ... or else *everybody* on Mining Station 3 had been in on the murder.

I left the room and glided through the cool, recycled air into the open circulation space and "swam" myself down to the airlock level at the bottom of the station, looking for some clue, something that would tell me what had happened here. I spent over two hours going over every square inch of the suit room and the red-edged inner airlock door, turning up nothing. I finally retreated to the bottom of the circulation space and just floated there in zero-gravity, staring across the suit room at the airlock and listening to the unbroken hum of the wall fans.

It was a different noise, however, something almost inaudible, that made me look up the circulation space soaring up above my head.

The outer walls of the circulation space had little metal balconies marking each of the six floors above the airlock level. I could not make out the unintelligible sound which had drawn my attention, but nearly 75 feet above I saw Yu on the topmost balcony, waving at me. I pushed myself into the clear and kicked off, sailing up in zero-g until I reached her level, just managing to catch myself at her balcony before I could sail past and slam into the ceiling. "What is it?"

"You took long enough," she said, rancor in her voice. "Do you know how long I've been shouting for you?"

"I was—"

"I've been looking for you for over an hour now! I was talking with Mr. Kaminski in the GeoLab—" she pointed at the balcony opposite us "—but he hadn't seen you. So I checked in with the Station Director—" she pointed up at the ceiling "—and she said you were interviewing Dig Team Two, so I went to see them—" she pointed off in yet a third direction "—but they had no idea where you were, and sent me back to Senior Staff. So I asked around and no one on the station had any idea where you were, so I just started yelling for you. Do you know how long I've been yelling for you? Why didn't you answer me? Are you trying to avoid me? It's because my uncle is the head of Research and Development, isn't it? I bet—"

"I wasn't deliberately avoiding you," I interjected—although, truth be told, I probably *would* have, if I'd know it was her. "I just couldn't hear you, all right? This isn't Mars, you know. The atmosphere in the station is at 5 psi, not 14-plus. In an atmosphere this thin, it's impossible for your voice to carry more than 30 feet or so. So I wasn't deliberately ignoring you, all right?" I let go a breath and braced myself for the verbal torrent. "What did you want me for?"

Her face grew excited. "I was thinking about the airlock accident. Do you know what 'inverse *déjà vu*' is? That's where surroundings appear unfamiliar when viewed from an unusual perspective. If the dig team floated down upside down into the suit room, they might not have recognized the airlock controls and hit the wrong button accidentally!"

I stopped her with a raised hand. "Which would make sense, if they were amateurs on their first trip out this airlock. But they weren't. They were trained professionals, and they'd used this airlock dozens of times. I'm pretty sure that they wouldn't have made a rookie mistake like inverse *déjà vu*."

Her face fell. "Oh."

As she frowned in concentration, I ran my hand through my hair. I was back to square-last, the one all the interviews had led me to. Either the lock had failed on its own, in which case no one was to blame ... or else the lock had been deliberately opened, in which case someone here was a killer. But they all had alibis that interlinked. So either no one was guilty...

...or everybody was.

And then it clicked. My eyes widened. Then I pointed at Yu. "Get everyone—you, Kaminski, the Senior Staff and *especially* Dig Team Two—gathered in the Mess hall. I've got something to show them."

. . .

I waited outside the Mess Hall with Kaminski, making sure that everyone else went in ahead of us. "Here," I said, slipping the geologist-auditor a snubgun. "The range is short, but it'll do for a chamber this small."

He froze, holding it like it was a live bomb. "What…?"

"I know who did it," I told him, keeping my eyes on the only door leading into the Mess Hall. "I'm going to make an arrest, but I'd prefer to have an ace in the hole in case things go south. You shouldn't need to use it, but if things get out of hand, make a show of force with it. That should be enough to keep things in hand."

He swallowed. "And if I have to shoot someone?"

"Aim for the center-of-mass. The bolts in that thing are pretty lightweight." I stepped to the door. "And for God's sake, keep your eyes on Dig Team Two!" I waved my hand over the entry sensor, and when the door dilated, I floated in with Kaminski following me.

The faux teakwood table was triangular; the five members of the Senior Staff floated on one side, their feet locked into black footholds on the deck—seats were a ridiculous waste of space and mass in zero-gravity. The five members of Dig Team Two all floated on the second side of the table, with their feet also locked into footholds in the deck. The third side had five empty footholds in the deck before it; the spots where Dig Team One would have put their feet. Yu positioned herself at the center of the empty five. I floated over to the empty foothold on the far right and maneuvered myself into place, Kaminski taking his place between me and Yu, his eyes tracking each of the members of Dig Team Two.

"So," I said pleasantly. "You're all here. Good."

Gonella frowned. "What's going on? What is it?"

"Five men are dead. I'm here to make arrest the killer. Or should I say '*killers*'?"

The ten members of the station stared at me in varying degrees of surprise, and then everyone protested all at once. Kaminski slid his hand into his jacket pocket, breathing hard, casting a sideways glance at me.

I gave an all-but-imperceptible shake of my head.

The ten kept on protesting, the miners the loudest of all. I raised a hand to them. "SHUT UP!"

The ten fell into silence, their eyes defiant.

I smiled. "The thing about this case was, every one of you has an alibi that seems... *seems*... to interlock with someone else's. In fact, all ten of you are each other's alibis. Which means that not one of you is guilty," I noted. "Or, you *all* are."

Gonella looked ill. "You—you can't be serious!"

"Can't I?" I asked. "Look at the facts: Dig Team One came in, refused to report what they had found on 19-Delta, and asked Central to send over a Geologist-Auditor. And everyone in this business knows what that means: a dig team had found something big, and wanted verification of what they found. That's why Kaminski was sent out here. So then someone here on Mining Station 3 decided that if there was a big strike, something really valuable, then Dig Team One shouldn't get to keep it. All *that* required was to pull a Jump Circuit console, install it in one of the main trunk lines, and send a remote signal to the airlock doors that overrode their safety protocols and made the outer door open while still under pressure. Afterwards, the JC-console got put away, and no one was the wiser. Five men dead, and it all looks like a freak accident. But there's one thing you didn't count on."

No one responded.

The station's engineer, Potemkin, finally cleared his throat. "What's that?"

"That someone might have been close enough to hear the last words of the dig team, right before the airlock blew out."

A look of shock circled the table.

I tossed my words at Kaminski while I kept my eyes on Dig Team Two. "Tell them what you told me."

Kaminski watched Team Two closely as he spoke. "I heard someone shouting, so I went out, and it turned out to be one of the miners. He yelled up to me that they were having a problem with the airlock, and I asked him what it was, and he called back that there was some kind of fault with the indicators for the main door. Then the airlock blew."

I smiled at the ten faces across the table from me. "You see? Ironclad evidence. That's how I knew Kaminski here was the murderer."

Every face at the table went into confusion, none more so than Kaminski's. He gaped at me, his mouth hanging open, and I glanced over at him. "Oh, that's right! This is your first time actually on a mining station out in the field, isn't it. Allow me to point out something: that unlike the labs at Ling Standard Central, the station atmosphere is 72% oxygen and just 28% nitrogen at 5 psi. It's a very workable solution to the problems of oxygen toxicity, but it has a side effect: the air is so thin that sound waves don't travel well. I know; I was in the suit room at the bottom of the circulation space and Yu was at the top of it yelling for me, only I couldn't hear her. That's because the air is so thin, it's impossible to make out what someone in the circulation space is saying if they're 30 or more feet away from you.

"And," I said, staring hard at the GeoAud, "the lab you were working in is at the top of the circulation space, a good 75 feet above the deck of the suit room. It's a physical impossibility that anyone on the GeoLab balcony could have heard what was being yelled up the shaft from the bottom level. So how is it that you managed to not only hear what the miner was saying, but even held a conversation with him?"

"I—" Kaminski gulped air, sweat dotting his pale face. He

pulled his feet free, grabbing hold of Yu and shoving the snubgun up against her head. "*Nobody move!*"

"You see?" I asked the table. "Ironclad evidence. So, what was it?" I asked the sweating GeoAud. "Gold? *Real* gold?"

Kaminski gritted his teeth. "No! Rhodium, in nickel ore. A huge vein of it. Massive. Billions of dollars' worth!" He grimly stared everyone down. "Now, I'm getting out of here."

"No you're not," I told him. "Oh, and before you go on about how you'll 'kill the girl' and then anyone else who 'gets in your way', let me just ask one thing. Do you think that gun I gave you is loaded?"

Kaminski's mouth hung open again, and then his face sagged. With a sick look of expectation he pulled the trigger, getting nothing but a click.

I drew my sidearm, which *was* loaded. "Geologist-Auditor Gregor Kaminski, under the auspices of the Space Control Act, Section 147, I arrest you for the crimes of murder in the first degree—"

After I got Kaminski locked up in the shuttle's cargo bay, I came back to finish my meeting with the personnel of Station 3, who waited in confusion. "How...?"

"It was something Yu said," I told them. "She mentioned that she had been talking with Kaminski in the GeoLab—which was directly opposite the balcony she was floating at when she kept shouting down for me. That's when I realized that Kaminski's entire story was a lie. His assay of the ore samples showed that Dig Team One had found a fantastically rich rhodium vein, and so he decided on the spur of the moment to kill them, make it look like an accident, and report to us that they had thought it might be pure gold, but instead had only found pyrite."

Gonella held her hand up. "But why? It's not like he could claim all that rhodium!"

"He didn't need to. You said it yourself, that Ling Standard would shut things down here and pull MS-3 back to Central for reassignment. That would leave Asteroid 19-Delta sitting off abandoned, with a false report going out that it held nothing but iron and pyrite."

Gonella's confusion grew palpable. "So?"

I tapped the faux wood tabletop, causing me to bounce slightly. "I searched his datafiles after the arrest. It turns out that even though he was on Ling Standard's payroll, he was also in the pay of the Butler Minerals Consortium; he's been sending copies of all of Ling Standard's geological reports to one of your competitors. He figured that once Ling Standard pulled MS-3 off this rock, he'd sell Butler Minerals the location of a certain asteroid filled with rhodium. And even if Ling Standard noticed a Butler-M ship out here attaching itself to 19-Delta, they'd laugh it off, thinking Butler was going to get nothing but useless pyrite. By the time anyone back at LSCC figured out that the airlock accident was no accident—assuming they ever did—Kaminski would be long gone with his multi-million dollar payoff and we'd never see him again."

The survivors of Kaminski's murder spree all nodded, whereas Yu just looked at me with surprise. "Do you know what the odds against that were? That's like something that should never have happened. But that's a good thing. The long odds, I mean. That means it'll never happen again!"

I kept my mouth shut, but I knew better. I'm a cop. The one thing I know for certain is that it'll happen again.

As long as humans are Human, it'll happen again.

FABIO-14 (ETC.)

T.E. ACKERSON

< *Damn carbon-muncher.* >

Grrrzwlt turned one eyestalk to the freshly dug almost-crater-size hole and his other to the trampled path that led through his field of young shimmery-red ferro-stalk. He let go a grumbling sigh as he contemplated the damage.

< *Almost caught him in the act this time.* >

Emerson Palmer kept very still, with only enough of his space helmet above the edge to allow himself to watch his "neighbor." The squattish red-hued alien wearing denim coveralls whipped his eyestalks to and fro.

Excitable sort, thought Emerson, as he crept down out of view and back to his own property. He stood up, switched his suit lights back on, and aimed one at his opened gloved palm. A marble-sized diamond-opal radiantly glowed back at him.

"Not a bad day," he said, smiling.

Fabio-14 (and a bunch of other numbers and letters) is a flattish six by eight kilometer asteroid, vaguely resembling a lumpy mango pit. It is a fragment of the boundary between the molten iron core and rocky crustal layer of a long-destroyed planet, giving it, respectively, a rusty red hue on one side (where the Palmer family lives) and a bright moonscape on the other (where the Grrrzwlt family lives). The asteroid is highly suitable for ferro-stalk (or ironweed as it is commonly known), a plantlike bio-nanite, needing only sunlight and a source of iron oxide to grow. Fabio-14 (etc.) slowly rotates on its long axis, giving it a 'day' and 'night', and even has a 0.5 gravity.

Emerson clumped out of the airlock and over to the de-con booth. He was still in there a half hour later, degaussing the last of the iron-weed and dust out of the suit's magnetics. Serena Palmer, his wife, leaned against the doorway, holding her ever present mug of steaming stinkwater (as he liked to call it.)

"Find anything?" she asked, taking a sip of her herbal drink. "Besides more iron-weed?"

"Just a small one," he replied. "Would have found more, but had to run. Still, it'll pay for air 'n water for the next six months." He swept up a small pile of iron bits and sand and dumped it into a bucket. "Can't figure out what they see in this stuff."

"It's gourmet to our neighbors, kind of like asparagus is to us, so don't throw it out."

Grrrzwlt was walking past the doorway of the machine barn when he glimpsed the furtive (and familiar!) ducking of a pair of eyestalks. He sidled up to a stall and peered over a divider. His two [children] sheepishly looked back at him.

< What do you have there, [boy]? >

[Boy] made no effort to hide an open tool box. He shrugged, picked out an adjustable wrench, and proceeded to lick at it like it was a lollipop. < We found it lying out in a field. >

< Uh-huh. >

[Girl-child], feeding a screwdriver to an eyestalked [iron-piggy] while giving it a neck scratch around it's enviro-field collar, gave him an innocent look that he knew was anything but. < *Gets that from her [mother]*, > he chuckled to himself.

[Boy] slurped away at his wrench. < I brought back another three cubic *zirgs* of dirt. I added it to the back berm. >

< Good. That will help with the orchard. > Grrrzwlt fished some ratchet wrench sockets from the box and popped them into his mouth. < *mmm, chromey!* >

< Well, don't let this spoil your dinner. And don't tell your [mother]! > He gave them a wink and left them to dispose of the evidence.

Grrrzwlt passed through the airlock seals before turning off his enviro-field. The wash of free flowing air over his [face] was always refreshing. The enviro-field was an advanced protective shield and life support system that worked very efficiently with the alien's iron-dense physiology (and not at all with an iron-poor human's.)

< How are the crops growing, [term of endearment]? > asked his [wife].

< Steady growth, though I found another hole in one of the patches. > he replied.

< About that. The [children] watched a [video] that you might be interested in. You have time to see it before [dinner]. >

He watched a small furry mam-mall creature (a 'skurl') with a fluffy tail scamper and gambol about, digging holes and alternately burying or retrieving small orbs of food. The hitherto odd behavior of his also mam-mall neighbor began to make sense.

The next morning, starting his rounds before sunrise, Grrrzwlt promptly fell into a freshly dug hole.

Emerson spent most of the day meandering around, prospecting his property. All he had found were some oddly shaped pieces of iron shale that could be turned into gift shop tchotchkes. And also more clumps of ironweed, which seemed to be popping up everywhere lately. Reaching his "front" porch, he turned to catch the sunset beyond the distant reddish hills.

One of which was now missing.

[Boy] brought the hover-tractor in for a perfect, smooth landing, his head nodding along with the music playing in his earbuds. Grrrzwlt approached as the vehicle powered down.

< Where's the trailer? >

[Boy] said < Whuht? > as his eyestalks looked confusedly behind him.

They found the trailer, and its cargo of iron-rich soil,

splashed across the pale landscape. The tow bolt had apparently snapped, though there were suspicious indications that it may have been sawn part way through...

Grrrzwlt gingerly hopped over to his side of the asteroid.

< Ow! Ow! Ow! >

He had been harvesting a rich clump of ferro-stalk on Em-er-son's side (it always grew better there! Which is why he had been throwing handfuls of seed into unobtrusive spots), when his neighbor discovered him.

And shot at his *feet* as he chased Grrrzwlt back to his own property.

Emerson literally half-dragged himself back inside, because only half of his spacesuit was still working.

Serena, with her ever-present mug of stinkwater, gaped at him in alarm. "What's the matter? Did you have a stroke?"

"No, nothing of the sort! Neighbor shot me with a stunner, whole left side of my suit's frozen up!" He unclipped his helmet.

"I thought we agreed that you wouldn't sneak over there anymore!"

"Welll..." he said, embarrassed, and pointed to his immobile left hand with his right.

Serena pried open his glove and found two small diamond-opals. She gave him a stern look, placed the gems in one of her pockets, and proceeded to put on her own spacesuit.

"What are you doing?" he asked.

"Something that should have been done a long time ago. I'm

going to the Outpost. Need to do some shopping. Have to make a stop first, though."

"What about me?" He gestured at his own disabled suit.

"You, you stay *inside* until I get back!" She grabbed the bucket of iron scraps, and lugged it toward the airlock.

"Hello, Mrs. Grrrzwlt," Serena said, offering up the bucket, stems of iron-weed arranged in a bouquet. "Do you have a moment?"

Soon after, they left for the Outpost, a day's flight away. < Going shopping, > explained Mrs. Grrrzwlt.

(Later, at their respective residences...)

"Honey, we need to talk."

< [Term of endearment], there is a discussion we must have. >

Months later, Emerson stood on the edge of Fabio-14 (etc.), waiting as Grrrzwlt ambled over.

"Hiya, Girzzy! How are you doing? Your crops seem to be doing well!"

< Hello, Em! > Grrrzwlt gestured toward a field of tall ferro-stalk, then stretched his arms and eyestalks up and waggled them. < Growing higher than an [oophalant]'s eye! > He pointed to the field of systematic holes on Palmer's side (it reminded him of the skurl). < Looks like you've been busy, too! >

Emerson held up a small gem. "I get lucky sometimes," he grinned.

< I tried to eat one of those once. Pretty bland. I hope you are finding enough to consume. >

"Oh, one of these goes a *long* way in keeping us fed, believe you me."

< I'll stick with my ironge orchard. They are a lot [tastier]. > Grrrzwlt winked.

"Sorry again about any trouble I caused. Things were really getting crazy for a while."

< Oh, it's oh-kay. It's fortunate the [wives] worked out a solution in time. >

"Yeah, sneaking off to the Outpost and filing to switch our land deeds caught me by surprise, but it's working out." He'd never mentioned that Serena had used his two gems for bribes to expedite the bureaucratic process.

< For us both. >

They nodded to each other in agreement, and looked upon their respective properties with satisfaction.

FRAGILE

MISHA BURNETT

I USED to run traffic control on Psamathe, a tiny little rock about as far from Neptune as Mercury is from the sun, which was given the title of moon mostly for convenience. It was a good vantage point for watching the outer system, though.

Back then pretty much all of the traffic in my corner of the sky was headed to Triton, loaded with supplies for making it into another pint-sized copy of Earth like they'd already done with Europa and Titan and Ganymede. Tucked in a corner of the occasional transport, though, was a package for me. Food and canisters for the air and water recyclers, mostly. I could have been more self-sufficient, but since I was just an auxiliary traffic-control station for a construction project it was easier to resupply me than to set up a closed ecology.

Most of the transport pilots saw making a second stop in Neptune orbit as a pain in the ass, and I couldn't blame them. It added a couple of days to what was already one of the longest hauls in the system, and they didn't get much of a bonus for my tonnage.

Captain Allison Sparks of the *Leatherstocking*, was an exception. She always seemed happy to drop off my cargo before she started the long fall back towards the sun.

"*Leatherstocking* to Psamathe," she called. "You awake, Bobby?"

I locked in on her transmission and cut in the beacon. "I hear you, Cap. You got some groceries for me?"

"Roger that, Psamathe," she said. "I've got sixty-two tons of pork rinds, special delivery."

I laughed. Allison's last trip had brought a load of fetal pigs in suspended animation to Triton, to be raised as food for the workers there. She was from Earth and assured me that fried pig skin was a delicacy there. I had my doubts. Like most working folks this far from the inner system, I hadn't much experience with mammal protein, but skin tissue didn't sound appetizing to me, no matter how it was prepared.

"Copy that, *Leatherstocking*," I checked my boards. "We have a lock. Assuming control now."

"Oh, I just love dominant men," Allison teased. She sounded sexy. I'd never seen her face, but her voice was pretty.

"You've got eighty-one minutes to enjoy it," I said, checking my board.

"So when are you going to put in for some leave and let me take you home with me?" she asked.

"Eh, I don't want to let anyone else run my planet. They wouldn't put things away and leave a big mess."

"Psamathe's not a planet." She always said that.

"It's inhabited," I gave her my usual reply. "By extra-terrestrial law, that makes it a planet."

"Hell, boy, I've had dogs bigger than that rock," she said.

"That is no way to talk to a Planetary Emperor," I told her.

"Emperor?" A laugh. "I thought you were going to set up a democracy."

"Naw, I got scared I might vote myself out of office. An absolute monarchy seemed safer."

"So you need an empress then," she said, that sexy edge coming back into her voice. "To ensure the succession."

"Oh, I've got one," I assured her. "You brought her in my last shipment. I just haven't gotten around to putting her together yet."

"Decided that you didn't want a robot on the throne?"

"No, it wasn't that," I replied, "I just told the factory I liked Asian girls, and they sent me the instructions in Chinese."

"There's no substitute for flesh and blood," she insisted.

"Don't knock it until you've tried it."

"Oh, I've tried it," and she was definitely flirting now, almost purring, "it's a long way back to civilization from here."

"Didn't like it?" I teased.

"I liked it just fine, but the damned batteries wore out before I got past Jupiter."

I laughed.

"You know," she said slowly, "I'm running over the top on the way back to miss the rings."

I sighed and checked the board. Time to get back to work. Allison was going to need a course home, after all.

The local plane of the elliptic was full of junk—as full as Saturn's rings, just not as pretty. That was the whole point of my station, to monitor the wreckage of what had been either three or four normal sized moons—cosmologists were still arguing that point—before tidal stresses broke them up.

So ships leaving my little world usually charted a course over the pole and then used Neptune's mass to swing them sunward through the relatively empty space above the planet's Northern latitudes.

I started the program running the numbers to give her computer.

"I could stick around for a while," she said.

"Huh?" I wasn't sure what she meant. Yes, it would be possible for her to remain in Psamathe orbit before heading up over Neptune, but why? It wasn't as if she'd be getting a boost to her acceleration from my orbital velocity—I took *twenty five years* to get around Neptune.

"Maybe I could spend some time on Psamathe," she said. "You know, see the sights."

I laughed at that, looking around my living space. Two big spheres and one little one, a dozen meters below the frozen methane surface. From where I drifted in my office I could see the whole of my bedroom (the other big sphere) and my bathroom (the little one).

"Well," I said, "it's tough to get reservations on such short notice, you know. This being our busy season and all."

"We could spend some time together," she said, and the invitation in her tone was unmistakable.

Oh, *shit*. She was serious.

I closed my eyes and scrubbed my face—very gently—with my hands.

"That's not a good idea," I said softly.

"I'm not asking you to marry me," she said, "just, you know, have some laughs."

"Allison, I have EOI," I said flatly.

"Oh." Dead silence for several seconds. Then, "I'm sorry. I didn't know." She sounded very sad.

Of course she didn't know. How could she? I'd never mentioned it. Maybe I should have, but I'd never taken our flirtation as anything more than two people killing time on a long, boring job. I'd been assuming that it was the same thing for her.

"Don't worry about it," I told her. "It's not a big thing."

That was a lie, of course. Environmental osteogenesis imperfecta was a *very* big thing. It had almost kept the human race from colonizing the solar system.

Today of course it seems obvious; but in the system's early days, space medicine was mostly a list of things to avoid. Don't look directly at the sun, don't go outside without a suit, things like that. Everybody knew, of course, that terrestrial biology was shaped by the fact that it was *terrestrial*. Things that live on Earth are adapted to Earth conditions. Simple, right?

But the details were fuzzy.

When Deimos Prime went truly self-sufficient it was seen as the biggest evolutionary leap since leaving the oceans back in the Whatchamacallit Era millions of years ago. The human race was living off the planet, raising food, generating power, making their own air and water and, in time, having babies.

Then six out of ten of those babies died in their first year. And those that survived were cripples.

From my perspective, decades later in my vantage point at the ass-end of nowhere, it can be hard to be charitable. They wasted years trying to pin down the syndrome to some dietary deficiency or radiation effect. There was a search for an infectious agent—there in the most sterile environment ever constructed. Some researchers went so far as to suggest that it was caused by a lack of some bacteria or virus common Earth that they had failed to bring with them to Mars orbit.

All the time the answer was just outside the windows, hanging there fourteen thousand miles away.

Gravity.

They'd known about muscle and skeletal deterioration from prolonged weightlessness since the first Earth orbital flights over a century ago. Somehow, though, no one thought to wonder what weightlessness would do to a developing child in the womb. I guess they figured that since the baby was already floating in fluid, it wouldn't make any difference.

Wrong.

These days, of course, a woman who gets pregnant in space

is quickly shipped back to Earth or to one of the colonies that has enough spin to provide a close approximation of one G. But they didn't do that when my mother was pregnant with me.

By the time that I was born they had a name for my condition even though they hadn't figured out what caused it. Environmental osteogenesis imperfecta, or EOI.

Brittle bone disease.

It existed on Earth, but there it was caused by a rare genetic anomaly—which maybe was why they spent so long barking up the wrong tree when it showed up in babies born in space. They could make braces for my arms and legs and teach me exercises designed to help my muscles compensate for my weak bones. When I reached my full growth—just a smidge over seven feet tall—I had surgery to implant titanium rods next to my long bones as internal braces.

But there is no cure. Once the skeleton starts growing—by about the thirteenth week of gestation—it's too late to fix it.

"I'm fine," I continued to fill Allison's embarrassed silence, "so long as I stay away from gravity."

"And acceleration," she said softly, "I guess."

I nodded and then since she couldn't see me I added, "Yeah. A tenth G is about my limit."

"And... people?"

"People make me nervous," I admitted.

"Because they could hurt you."

"It's not that I think people want to hurt me," I said quickly, "Not on purpose. People aren't monsters."

"But you're so fragile," she finished for me. "I understand." Very sadly.

I checked my board. The *Leatherstocking* was nine minutes out. Time to suit up.

"You're getting close," I told her. "I need to go meet the container. I've got an empty for you, too."

"Copy that, Bobby." All business again. Good.

I wore a Waldo404 powerloader on the surface—way more suit than anyone else would need for Psamathe's pathetic one percent of a G field. But it was the cheapest one on the market with a full rigid exoskeleton. Inside it I became unbreakable.

I had to be careful to make sure I kept the magnetic grapples on, though. The escape velocity of my kingdom was about only thirty feet per second. A good jump could win me an all expense paid trip to Uranus on a long orbit.

Leatherstocking drifted down gently and Allison cut in her own grapples so skillfully that I barely felt the click of contact through my suit when she locked into place. She was a heck of pilot—some tug jockeys slammed into the rock like they were trying to reposition its orbit.

The cargo hatch slid open and I clanked inside. The supply container was nearly as big as my entire habitat, but it was lost inside *Leatherstocking's* hold. I clipped onto it and slid it out, moving nice and slow, as its mass required. I clamped it down on my landing pad and with a start I saw the empty container was in motion.

I felt a jolt of fear that the grapples had failed and it was on an uncontrolled skid—even empty, the container was massive enough to flatten me or even damage the *Leatherstocking*, if it had any velocity behind it and hit something vital.

Then I looked again. It wasn't uncontrolled; a figure in a pressure suit was towing it. Allison? A pilot going outside and moving cargo?

It was unheard-of. Almost easier to believe that I had been visited by some native Neptunian form of life that had randomly decided to make itself known to the human race by assisting in loading a tug.

But it *was* Allison. I opened the short-range channel on my suit.

"You don't have to do that," I protested. "I'm wearing a Waldo."

"Just take a minute," she said, "Don't tell the union, okay?"

She moved like a flatlander, keeping her body at right angles to the surface as if she were standing up, but she handled the container well. I stood back and let her slide it into position in the hold.

She looked good doing it, too. Her body had that heavy roundness women get from fighting gravity all their lives. Her pressure suit was unarmored, a formfitted second skin that left very little to the imagination.

It also, I realized, didn't offer anything close to the kind of insulation she needed. In the shadow of Neptune we were at the next best thing to absolute zero, and she was radiating body heat like a furnace.

"Hey," I said, "you need to get back inside. Thanks and all, but you don't have the gear for this."

She turned to face me before replying—another Earthism—and said, "Are you going to invite me in for a drink?"

I thought it over for a second. It had been a long time since I had been face to face with anyone, much less a pretty girl. Fear and excitement battled inside me. Excitement won.

"Come on," I said. "Follow me, and keep your grapples on."

I went down the metal path to my airlock, thinking over my store of supplies. I could offer her a bubble of wine—made from Ganymede apples, very sweet—and I had a pretty fair selection of snacks. I was out of practice at being a host, but I could wing it.

When the lock was done cycling I cracked open the Waldo and slithered out. Allison pulled off her helmet and backpack and stuck them to the wall. Her breath suddenly quickened and she turned to me, eyes wide.

"I don't think this is tight," she gasped, grabbing for her helmet again.

I launched myself through the inner door and into my living space. "Hang on," I told her over my shoulder. "I keep the O2 pressure low in here. I'll raise the mix."

She looked dubious, but left her helmet where it was and followed me in. My standard pressure was 600 mbar. I dragged the slider to 1000 mbar and heard the blowers change in pitch.

"Give it a minute," I said. I was already feeling it.

"Thanks," she said, then worked her jaws as she looked around my office. She was lovely, strong and lush. I tried not to stare, feeling suddenly awkward. No one other than me had been in this space since the Colonial Authority techs had built it, six years ago.

"How about some wine?" I suggested, and went into my sleeping sphere without waiting for an answer. She was looking at the panorama screens in my office, watching the dance of junk around Neptune. It was an impressive display, to be honest, bigger than most ship's screens, and could be overwhelming.

I grabbed two squeeze bubbles and filled them with apple wine. I drink it chilled, which would horrify the Ganymede Vintner's Association.

When I came back Allison had a gun in her hand, pointed in my direction.

"Uh." I said. Then, "Is that a gun?"

She nodded, then cocked her head to the side. "Not that I really need it with you," she said thoughtfully.

All of a sudden she was a whole lot less pretty.

I floated in the doorway, my two bubbles of wine in my hands. "Why?"

"Well, I could just break you with my hands, couldn't I?" she replied.

"No, I mean why are you pointing a gun at me?" I asked. It

didn't seem real. Not the gun, that seemed very real. It looked just like the ones that the Colonial Authority cops carry. But I couldn't figure out what she wanted with me. "Is this a robbery? Because most of what I have was in your hold until half an hour ago. You could have just kept it."

She stuck the gun back in her thigh pocket. She was right, with her one-G muscles and my brittle bones there was no way I could fight her. "No, we're just going to sit here for a couple of hours and do nothing."

"I don't get it," I said.

She glanced at the display on her suit forearm. "Two and a half hours. Then I'll be gone." She looked back at me. "I really am sorry about this. I had hoped that I could just... distract you."

I took a drink from one of the bubbles of wine.

"Oh," she smiled, but I didn't find it as fetching as she'd intended. "May I?"

I tossed her the other bubble and she snagged it. After she'd had a sip she said, "You're right, this is good."

"What happens in two and a half hours?" I asked.

"I leave," she said. "That's all."

She looked up at my system display again and then I did get it.

Psamathe was positioned at the far edge of Neptune's ring system. I had a view of every possible approach to Triton and any ship coming or going—that was the whole point of my station. Allison, or someone she was working for, wanted to do something in Neptune's shadow without anyone knowing about it. Planning on hijacking a supply ship? Probably. There were hundreds of millions going into the terraforming project.

Which meant that no matter what she said now, she couldn't afford to leave me alive when she left. I knew too much already. I was only alive now in case someone called me and she needed me to answer it, to keep anyone from getting suspicious.

Unless I did something about it, I had two and a half hours to live.

I caught her eyes. She was looking intently at me, watching me work it out.

I forced a smile. I needed to make her think I believed her fairytale about leaving me alive and unharmed when she went back to the *Leatherstocking*. What would I say if I did?

"I see," I said slowly. "Any chance of getting a cut of the take?"

That was the right answer. I saw her face relax into a smile. "Something might be worked out," she said coyly. "What did you have in mind?"

She answered me quickly enough to let me know I had been right. She had no intention of letting me live.

I drifted a little closer, took another sip of wine. I hoped it would keep my hands from shaking. "I don't need much. But if this comes back on me and I lose this job I could use a nest egg."

Her eyes were cold and for a moment I thought I had gone too far. Then she nodded. "Fair enough. I can have my friends set up a bugout account for you once the job's done."

I glanced up at the screen and then deliberately turned my back to it. Facing her I said, "That'll work. So... you want some lunch while we're waiting?"

Again that smile, warm and seductive. I wasn't buying it, though. "Sure. That would be nice."

I went back into my sleeping sphere, thinking furiously. She'd never let me get close enough to my comm panel to put out a distress call.

Automatically my hands went through their motions, throwing some meatballs in my boiler and latching it, connecting the water inlet and pumping up the pressure—the pressure was too high.

Oh, right. I'd raised the ambient to Earth sea level standard to make Allison more comfortable.

Bitch. I should have cranked it down the other way and suffocated her. Too late now, she'd stop me from getting to the environmental panel, too. And even if I could reach it, she'd just break my arms and reset it. It took time to adjust the pressure. *Unless...*

Then I had it. I didn't like my odds, but I figured it was the only way I had any chance at all.

I waited until my boiler was done and then vented it, cracked it open, and scooped the meatballs into a dish and closed it up. Drifted back into the office.

"Here," I offered.

"Thank you," she said. She opened the dish and popped one in her mouth. After chewing she said, "You're taking this well."

I shrugged. "What else can I do?"

She smiled. It wasn't a nice smile, but she thought it was. "Smart boy."

"Okay if I hit the head?" I asked.

She nodded, chewing again.

I went into my bathroom, slid closed the door. Then I popped open the electrical panel on the wall. The bus breakers had plenty of current for what I wanted, but I needed metal. Frantically I looked around. Toothbrush, shampoo, even my razor—all plastic. I spied the knob for the shower. If I could get that loose...

I pulled, then took a deep breath, braced myself, and pulled harder. I felt a bright burst of pain in my hand as something snapped, but the knob was free in my hand. Wincing, I grabbed a towel from the dispenser to wrap around my hand, then pressed the knob to the breakers, shorting across the biggest two.

There was a flash. Smoke rolled out of the panel. A moment later the strobes kicked in and a horn sounded.

"Fire warning," said my computer in a calm voice. "Fire has been detected. Emergency atmosphere purge initiated."

Allison was pounding on the door. *"Bobby, what did you do?"*

I wedged myself against the door but I knew I wouldn't be able to hold it for long. She yanked from the outside. Then I felt her shifting position to get more leverage. I waited until she tugged and threw it open in her face. She went spinning off one way, I launched myself the other.

The blowers were howling, drawing streamers of smoke across the office to the vents.

She oriented herself fast and pushed off towards me. We collided and I kicked off hard—too hard. I slammed into the wall and felt ribs giving, pain robbing me of breath. But I had to keep moving.

She had bounced off the opposite wall and was headed at me again. Even though she was a flatlander, she was a pilot and used to zero-G maneuvers. I wouldn't be able to keep away from her forever.

Fortunately, I didn't have to.

She was already gasping for breath. Fire protocol for a station like mine was simple—pump out the oxygen and replace it with nitrogen, smothering the fire. She realized what was happening and left off chasing me to bound towards the airlock door, heading for her helmet and tanks. I got there first and locked down the safeties, then bounced away again. I was starting to feel light headed myself. I hoped that I could stay conscious long enough.

Allison passed out before she got the door open.

I went to the environmental panel and overrode the fire alarm, set ambient back to 600 mbar. The smoke was mostly gone. I'd have to replace the breakers in the bathroom, but that could wait.

My ribs were screaming at me and my hand wasn't good for

much. That was okay; I used my good hand to tow her to the wall and went through half a tube of hull sealant caulking her in place. Once it set it would take a torch to free her.

I called Triton, requesting police and medical assistance. Then I ran a scan and located a dull shape, far too hot to be a local rock, hiding in the shadow of Nereid. A ship, probably a tug, sitting with its drive off.

"Hey!" Allison called, struggling against the sealant holding her in place, but it was hard set by then.

I turned to look at her. Waited for her to realize that she wasn't getting out under her own power. Eventually she did.

She sighed. "What happens now?"

I shrugged. "That kind of depends." I highlighted the ship I'd found. "I'm guessing this is your friends?"

She looked at the display, then back to me.

"I'm sure we can work out some kind of deal," She said, trying a seductive smile.

"Don't," I told her. "Just don't. It's way too late for that, now."

Her face got serious. "Okay, let's talk money."

I shook my head. "Too late for that, too. There's no way I can trust you. The question is, can your friends trust you?"

She looked puzzled.

I explained. "Right now they're just guilty of failing to file a flight plan and running without a beacon. All they're going to get is a fine. Maybe the pilot will lose his license if they decide to throw the book at him and he's got priors. You, on the other hand, are looking at some serious time for assault. Doesn't seem fair, does it?"

She frowned.

"Triton's got a ship on its way. I haven't told them about the tug in Neried's shadow yet, and I won't mention it unless it moves. I figure that'll give you something to bargain with."

She seemed about to say something else, but just shook her head. She didn't talk to me again.

I spent a week in hospital on Triton.

While I was there they told me that Allison had given up the others, filling the Colonial Authority in on the whole plan. She ended up doing her time in a Martian work camp. The crew of the tug, on the other hand, got sent up for attempted piracy. Last I heard they had been sent to the Death Valley supermax. The CA takes piracy *very* seriously.

After I got out of the hospital they gave me the option to stay and I took it. Someone else got to be the emperor of Psamathe and I ran a loader for Logistics & Supply. At first it was tough to get out of the suit at the end of my shift. I felt vulnerable, exposed. But you can't hide away forever.

Allison had taught me that.

I went outside with everybody else on O2 Day, when the atmosphere was certified breathable. It wasn't much of an event, honestly, a couple of speeches and a band and a crowd standing around under the sky. But it was a big deal at the time.

It still is, when I think about it.

After the colony officially opened I invested in an orchard with a few partners. We do okay. I put on some weight, gained muscle mass.

They replaced the human operator on Psamathe with one of the new generation AIs. It doesn't need food or air, doesn't sleep, and nobody flirts with it.

I got a message from Allison. She'd served her ten years and got full Martian citizenship, got married and had a baby girl. She sent me a picture of her girl, a cute little thing in a polka-dot jumper, playing in the sand.

I never wrote back. I couldn't think of what to say.

But I kept the picture.

THE SHOT LAUNCHED AROUND THE WORLD

GEOFFREY HART

So we're on the surface of some asteroid too small to have a name—just some number only an astronomer could love. We're there to watch an ex-Olympian who never medaled, but who clearly became a gold medalist in self-promotion. Her name's Shere-something-African. Ruth, my pet journalist, knows; I'm just the cameraman, and after a time, the names and faces all blur and all you care about are (a) the lighting and (b) the inevitable photobombers, though I'm not expecting many this time. We're here to watch Shere launch a javelin (an event in which she placed 30th in the world) at just the right angle so it perfectly orbits this tiny airless world and returns to its starting point. As spectacle, it makes no sense, but it's part of a Red Bull commercial, so who expects sense?

Ruth presses her helmet's faceplate against mine. "Aren't you excited?"

I was excited when I was her age and she wasn't even a hungry gleam in her Mummy's eyes yet. "What's to be excited about?"

"This is history in the making."

"My first use of a zero-gee toilet was history in the making. It didn't make the news either."

She snorts. "But you're not an Olympian, and you're not a tradition."

"There's a tradition?"

"Yes. It dates back to the early 1970s. One of the Apollo missions." She pauses to consult her augments. "Yes: 1971, Apollo 14. There was this NASA astronaut, Edgar Mitchell, who just about died. He was supposed to be on the Apollo 13 mission, the one that was a complete near-disaster. But they bumped him to the next mission."

Complete near-disaster? "So two events makes a tradition these days?"

"I guess. Anyway, he was a competent astronaut—back then, even NASA didn't hire incompetents—but a bit of a whack job. Mister *we are stardust, we are golden*, they called him. The point is, he has the record for being the guy who launched the first 'javelin' on the moon—actually, the first javelin outside Earth's atmosphere, which is probably more impressive since nobody's ever bothered trying to launch a javelin anywhere but Earth since then."

"So you're telling me NASA spent a gazillion taxpayer dollars to put a javelin on the moon? That must have been popular."

"No, they weren't that frivolous. It was actually a tool handle of some sort. It just *looked* like a javelin. In any event, Alan Shepard trumped him by smuggling a golf club aboard the lander and becoming the first golfer on the moon. Nobody remembers the javelin anymore."

"I see. Golf clubs. At least *that* isn't frivolous."

"Hush. Here she comes!"

Shere whatsername has emerged from the bus that brought us all here, and she's waving and pressing the flesh. Well, pressing the vacuum insulation, leastwise. You'd never know she's anyone special; all space suits look the same. But she does move with a certain lithe confidence the rest of us lack, so that's something; it looks great on the monitor. I've been recording automatically all along, but now I toggle my personal camera to manual. *This* will be the video without the network logo at the bottom right of the screen and without the advertising feeds at the top and bottom; this one I'll release on the darknet. Daddy's got expensive habits, and network journalism only pays for so much.

Which would be fine if the guys who loaned Daddy the money to pay for those habits were a bit more patient about repayment schedules. But they're not what you'd call patient, and that's why I'm here for this dumbass non-event. Dumbass or not, it pays well and there's a chance it will pay better if something goes wrong and I can capture it.

They've removed the surveyor's transit the scientists used to calculate the elevation and trajectory of the release, and I've captured Shere's gopher using a can of compressed air to remove all signs that it was ever there, erasing a billion years worth of dust accumulation to reveal the pockmarked surface that it concealed for a billion years. The crust is non-reflective space-black, and a bitch to light properly against a space-black background; thank God for shadows and specular reflection and modern smartlights.

Another gopher scuttles out of the darkness bearing a bag of javelins, each gleaming white so we can see them more easily. Shere makes a big show of weighing them, arm moving smoothly back and forth as if she hasn't already tested each one a hundred times to ensure it's the same as all the others to the nearest microgram. She could be throwing a flagpole for all it matters; without an atmosphere, this isn't rocket science.

"Bet you a piña colada she impales herself at the end of the orbit." But I'm looking at all the amateurs clustered around the launch site, or at least within the permitted distance. *Paparazzi.*

"Hush."

"Don't be a worrywart, Ruth. They'll fix it in post-production."

"*Hush!*"

I bite my tongue. I've already staked out one of the two best positions for watching Shere catch the inbound javelin, and nobody's moving me from this spot. It'll all be over soon, and I can decompress back at the ship's bar. Well, maybe decompress isn't the most auspicious word. Anyway...

Shere takes her mark, makes a show of planting her feet, crouching. She's already been out here twice, making sure she's got exactly the right release height. There won't be any run-up either; not enough gee, and it's not really about distance. But this girl's got camera sense, and she practices her movements in a way that'll make all the highlight reels. (Whatever a "reel" is. Short for *reality?*)

When she's ready, we hear her take a deep breath over the microphone; she pivots like she's riding on magnetic bearings and launches the javelin. Everyone watches as it soars past the horizon, arcing gently downwards and out of sight. It would be lost to sight entirely were it not for the camera drones trailing it, spewing clouds of exhaust gases to keep themselves in tight orbit around this chunk of rock.

We wait, literally cooling our heels, and then there's a collective intake of breath as the javelin tracker *pings*. Everyone faces the other direction, and sure enough, here comes the javelin. But she's put too much into her throw, and it's way overhead. No way she's going to catch this one, though I see her bending her knees as if she's thinking of jumping. Then she remembers where she is. Pity. Would have made a great shot watching her soaring off into the void and having to be rescued. Would have been great *money* in being persuaded to *not* broadcast that image.

The javelin disappears into the void, where it will undoubtedly endanger some future space mission, and she shrugs, waves at the cameras, and takes a second javelin from the gopher. Again, she preens for the camera, flexes, pivots, and launches the javelin. Again, it disappears below the horizon. We wait, the tracker *pings*, and we keep waiting. Nope. This time, *not enough* velocity; the javelin has buried itself in the dust several hundred meters away.

Shere shrugs, the gopher brings a third javelin, and again she goes through her routine. By now, I'm not optimistic, but this time it looks like she's got it right. The tracker *pings*, Shere minutely adjusts her stance as the javelin comes into view, and she reaches out in preparation to snag it—and at that precise moment, the paparazzo who's been waiting for the money shot steps into the frame.

His camera flashes, perfectly placed in case the star of the moment misses her catch. But he's an amateur and has misjudged his position: the javelin is headed straight for him.

He doesn't see it coming. The javelin is going to embed itself in his helmet or his vac suit, followed by a dramatic puff of air, pink-tinged in the glare of the camera lights, and he'll fly spinning off into the void, propelled by the momentum of the impact and his own personal exhaust. *Great* imagery.

But good though the money would've been, there are some things I won't do for money. *I'm* not a paparazzo, fer chrissake. So instead, I throw my backpack at him, catching him high enough in the chest to tip him backwards, out of frame—and more importantly, out of the javelin's path. My camera's been running ever since the toss, and neatly captures Shere-whatever catching the javelin, legs braced against a rock to absorb the momentum and keep her firmly grounded.

I wait for the nearly ex-photographer to finish his fall and bounce, then I turn off my personal camera and turn to my pet journalist.

"That's a wrap. And Ruth? I owe you a piña colada."

I can afford the drink. I'm thinking that even if the shots of the fall and bounce don't pay back those loans, they will at least be a decent down-payment. And I hear Red Bull's doing some kind of base-jumping event with guys in special suits diving into the atmosphere of a red giant star. That couldn't possibly end badly, could it?

RESONANCE

KENNETH B. CHIACCHIA

NORA ANGAVU IS DEAD. The rubble-pile silicate asteroid S38M9XD is vibrating.

These are the facts of the matter: the encoded telemetry of Angavu's skinsuit announcing her death, and the self-evident movement of the components of S38. All else is conjecture.

It might be more accurate to say that all else is hypothesis; for we do have evidence, and testimony, and instinct to go on. To say that Angavu's motivations are today not fully understood; to say that Madeleine Lapinski is missing; to question whether a small explosive device could create the effects observed on S38; these are not to say that we can never know the answers, we will never find out what happened. Only that we must resist the rush to judgment that both sides of this conflict have made.

We must start with the personalities involved. They are the elementary building blocks from which all else devolves. Joshua Goldman, 25 years old at the time, is barely describable as an "actor" in these events. Still, much hinged on his relationship with the 23-year-old Angavu. It's possible that if it weren't for this then-respectable young exobiologist's involvement, the radical astrogeologist would never have convinced Lapinski to accompany her on the asteroid "caving" trip.

I was unable to speak with Goldman himself; he has refused all contact with the media. Since he did not take the stand in his own trial, we do not have recourse to court records either.

"Josh had it bad," said Jinho Chen, secretary of the Facility 823 Grotto of the Interplanetary Speleological Society. "You'd tell him, guy, it's just not going to happen; and he'd pretend like he didn't know what you were talking about. She played him, sure."

Chen must have read my expression, because he said, "It wasn't like you're thinking, either. She wasn't cold about it: sometimes, like at a party and she didn't think anybody was looking, she'd *look* at him. Wasn't quite the kind of look he *wanted* her to have, no; but she cared for him. It was something real, whatever it was."

Angavu is the inevitable focus of the tale. I've seen the vids of her—more than just the ones released to the media, I've watched a number of private vids the cavers, who are even more casual about nudity than the usual run of spacers, made at their events. She was, without a doubt, a beautiful woman: deep black skin; striking, angled facial features; pleasing curves; magnificent locks of hair.

But Josh Goldman, a handsome, personable young man with a reasonably normal love life prior to meeting Angavu, knew other beautiful women as well. We have to look deeper than shallow attraction.

"She was a righteous woman," explained Eli823, one of the many followers that Angavu's reputed act of sabotage generated. "Of course he loved her."

For the record, I never actually met Eli—I confirmed he was real, but all of our interviews were conducted in time-shifted, image-altered fashion.

But what about the effects on S38? Didn't she in effect destroy the asteroid to save it?

"Crap," Eli told me. "She didn't destroy anything; S38 has been hit with bigger shocks many times in its history. When the reverberations die down, it will be exactly what it was before— a rubble pile. Only the geometry of the rubble will have changed. *That's* what she destroyed: cavers' passageways. She sacrificed what she enjoyed to save the asteroid from total destruction."

"Yeah, I've heard some of Eli's opinions," Chen responded. "All I can say is that Nora didn't make life any easier for us cavers. All of a sudden, we're all monkeywrenchers until proven otherwise."

Jack Iino, a spokesperson for Consolidated Orbital Recovery —which owns the Near-Earth Asteroid Pulverizing Plant, the "asteroid eater" that had been slated to digest S38—has some sympathy for Chen and what he calls "legitimate cavers." Not that he necessarily trusts them.

"There's an old saying," Iino said. " 'Every terrorist has a grievance, but not every grievance has a terrorist.' This community doesn't exactly have a spotless reputation for expressing its grievances appropriately; but he's right, it isn't fair to tar them all with what a few of them do. Not that the proposition that a lifeless chunk of rock needs to be conserved carries much weight with me, in the light of humanity's needs.

"Angavu chose to make a political statement with violence. Don't believe that nonsense about how she didn't hurt anybody but herself—the plan was to kill Madeleine when they disrupted the asteroid, Maddy only survived because something went wrong. Maybe Angavu never even intended to die. I'm still not so sure that these folks didn't get Maddy somehow. It's a little too pat how she disappeared."

Madeleine Lapinski, then 30, is the cipher of the story. She was there—if we are to believe Goldman—as a witness to the glory of the astro-cave environment. They wanted a convert.

"Well, that's the weakest part of the lie," Iino said. "Maddy never peeped a word of the kind of radicalism they espoused to anybody. I knew her, and I just don't buy that they thought they could 'turn' her. Let alone the other stuff they say."

"The other stuff" is among the most hotly debated aspects of the Nora Angavu mythology. To hear Eli and the other self-styled successors of Angavu's legacy tell it, her self-sacrifice *did* turn Madeleine Lapinski. She disappeared soon after the incident; some say she's one of the people sabotaging planetary development projects even now. One rumor even has it that she is Eli.

"No way," said Marco Serra, a short-haul interplanetary pilot who worked with Lapinski. "Look, it's not that complicated. She takes a couple of cavers into an asteroid her company is planning to develop, and they ruin it. I don't care how many reassurances the big guys give you, your career is over at that point. I'll bet she's still around, working somewhere that nobody knows her. Faces can be changed, ident codes can be faked. Somewhere far; someplace on Mars, or maybe the Triton facility. She's working, that's all. She's started a new life."

Renee Komossa, Lapinski's younger sister by two years, isn't sure what to think. "I don't know that I can recall anything like... like what they're saying today," she said. "Maddy wasn't the kind of person who was easily swayed. She either bought an idea or she didn't, I never saw anybody bully or wheedle her.

"Still, there was one time—we were just kids, I wasn't much more than ten or so—that she took me on one of her outings in City Six."

The family knew Madeleine was destined for space, Renee

said. Always the explorer, Madeleine had found an abandoned structure, buried under a few levels of newer construction near the core of one of the pre-City-Six metropolises. There the sisters ran around in a dilapidated building a century or more old —the kind of place that isn't supposed to exist anymore, let alone be accessible by two pre-adolescent children.

"I was terrified," Renee said. "You don't see this kind of thing outside of history vids; it had exposed, jagged metal, metal wires, broken glass. The buildings above and on either side of it couldn't have been resting on it, it would have caved, somebody must have built around it intending either to restore it or demolish it, and then forgot for some reason."

Then their father showed up.

"We had our communicators on us, so it was no surprise he found us. He was furious at Maddy—she was always the ring-leader. 'Why did you come here? Don't you know you could have been hurt?' He said there was a perfectly nice playground near our apartment, and if we didn't like the rides we could always VR anything we could imagine."

Renee's face took on a faraway look as she continued, "And Maddy looks him in the eye—always the bold one—and says, 'I don't always want something that was *made* for me,' she says. They gutted the place the next week—Daddy must have complained to somebody. Maddy cried and cried. I still don't have the slightest idea of what that was about. But I'll never forget that."

Still, whatever Madeleine Lapinski did or didn't do or say as a child, it seems an unlikely prospect that someone who was so grounded in the interplanetary-development world could be swayed simply by taking her caving inside a rubble-pile asteroid. At least, that's what I thought.

Then I visited S42G8FF, a small near-Earth asteroid similar to S38—and like S38, it is slated for digestion by the Near-Earth Asteroid Pulverizing Plant. Chen and a couple of the cavers from his grotto took me.

Asteroid caving is inherently dangerous. Oxygen regenerators have removed the potential hazard of running out of breathable air, but regenerators depend on a power source; and it is possible to run out of power. Also, despite the weak gravity, the rocks can be massive. In the open, it's easy to dodge a moving boulder. When you're hemmed in by multiple boulders, getting out of the way can be trickier than it sounds. "Live rock" can be so tenu-ously balanced under multiple, skewed forces that a relatively small bump can snap the collective assembly out of whack, trig-gering slow-motion void collapses that can kill cavers—and have.

Then there's the simple possibility of getting so badly stuck in a "squeeze" that you can't get out before your power supply runs down. Sometimes rescue equipment for "modifying" the rock can't be brought to you; sometimes your power leads are so inac-cessible that neither you nor your would-be rescuers can hook up replacement power modules.

We speak of "passages" within a rubble-pile asteroid, but that term is a bit of a construct. There are, of course, no real passages; there is only a three-dimensional pile of rocks that fit together imperfectly. Random voids in the pile, one man's passage is another's impenetrable crack. Getting through depends on size (many cavers are thin, though not all), technique, and a knack for wriggling through enclosed spaces without the help of gravity to generate friction.

Squeezes are, arguably, the most powerful experience in astro-caving. Normally you float through the passages slowly, carefully, hand-over-handing yourself along the rock. Through your skinsuit's intelligent membrane you can feel the rough, cracked texture of the rock rasp past. It's slippery, though: microscopic spheres of glass, produced by the collisions that made the rubble pile, slick your grip so that you have to be careful not to skid out of control—and maybe into live rock.

Unless you're very unlucky, the rock doesn't move. In a squeeze, though, it can seem otherwise. With rough stone crushing you from above and below, you sometimes have to exhale and employ a method called the pelvic tilt to flatten out in order to pass—you pull in your stomach, straighten the lower spine and rotate the plane of your pelvis in line. Men also must exhale, as they tend to stick at their chests—women are more likely to catch at the hips.

You have to ignore a little pain; setting the skinsuit so that you don't feel the abrasion at all would deprive you of the sensitivity you need to manage your movement. The automatic padding around your torso spares you the worst of the scraping there, though you can still feel it.

Move carefully: the rock can and will tear the membrane of your skinsuit. The suit is self-healing, so the exposure to vacuum would be momentary and not harmful, except in the case of the most major breaches. But the deafening pop and hiss will scare the piss out of you, believe me.

If your safety line gets wedged between you and the rock, it can dig painfully into your hip. Intelligent materials try to manage the length and positioning of the line, but it can still get in the way—and if you panic, you can tangle yourself so badly that the AI doesn't know how to reconfigure it.

You need that line, though. One of the components of a rubble-pile asteroid is a fine dust, pulverized by the catastrophic processes that created the pile. As you pass, the thickness of this dust varies; at times it's barely noticeable. Other times, your passage kicks up thick, gray clouds that swallow your helmet lamp's beam and make the line necessary simply to orient your-self. Of course, because of the microgravity, the cloud doesn't settle—not on anything like a human time scale.

Chen taught me a trick in which you use the thrust from your propulsion unit to fill the immediate space with exhaust gases. That pushes the dust out, back along the hundreds of gaps and cracks, large and small, which surround you. It's not a technique for when you're tangled and panicked, though. If you don't wedge your back securely against a big, flat, stable rock, the thrust from the unit can send you—or worse, the rocks you hit —flying.

Rarely, you'll run across a big void. Names like "The Hall of the Mountain King," "Grand Canyon," and "Vast Void" grace ISS maps of asteroid passageways. For me, these features carried even more emotional impact than the squeezes.

When you emerge from a squeeze into a big void, you have to switch your lamp to floodlight mode—the darkness would swallow the gentle glow favored for tight passageways. Through a silent haze of dust, brilliant light fills an elongated chamber defined by hundreds of jagged, cracked, brownish rocks. Again, it has no real walls; only a lattice of holes of varying sizes.

I don't know how Lapinski reacted to her first sight of a void. I know I floated there for more than five minutes without saying a word. My mouth hung open the whole time—Chen pointed that part out to me later, with some glee.

No, the experience didn't make me take up with astro-terror-ists. Still, I wasn't entirely comfortable with some of the things that I felt, that I thought, floating in the void. I wonder what the presence of a true prophetess like Angavu would have done.

That is why I wouldn't discount the rumors of Lapinski turning on her erstwhile employers.

Most of the commentators, it seems to me, have treated this as essentially a problem in motivational logic—if past history and motivation wouldn't have led one to believe Lapinski could turn astro-terrorist, why would she?

But we're not talking about logic, or even run-of-the-mill emotion. We're talking about religion. I can explain it in no other way. We held no overt rituals, partook of no explicit sacraments when Chen and his friends took me "in cave." Yet something profound passed between us. I suspect that there is, within some of us, a howling thing that greets the wild as kin—a deep need to keep wildness close to us, regardless of the cost.

Those who elect to live in Preserve Earth, who voluntarily cast aside so many of the technologies that the bulk of humanity cannot do without, are an example of this. What I'm talking about, though, is purer, more potent.

Conservation on Earth always had fuzzy animals as its rallying point. Many of those who gave their money, their time, and even their blood to save natural ecosystems possibly did so in a willful misunderstanding of what they were saving. Deep in the bowels of a rock pile floating in space, there can be no thought of communing with creatures, or even of self-interested conservation. There is nothing in a rubble pile to make friends with, nothing that a person (as opposed to a corporation) can use: only wildness. You either resonate with that or you don't.

Madeleine Lapinski either resonated with it or she didn't. I'm not so sure that even the people who knew her best would have seen that part of her before it was tested.

Of course, I've been carrying out my own kind of willfulness up until now, in avoiding a major point of controversy regarding the S38 incident: could any explosive device that Nora Angavu carried into S38 produce the gravitational resonance that we now see? Certainly, despite a number of sabotage incidents by her would-be followers, no one has managed to repeat the feat. They've been bloodier, but never as big.

First, the theory: since a rubble-pile asteroid is held together only by the loose mutual gravitational attraction of its components, it should be possible, with a properly placed explosion, to disrupt the connections that hold them in their initial geometry.

Once those contacts are gone, the rocks fall inward under the force of gravity, collapsing some of the voids. Then they impact each other; the recoil from that impact then sends them outward again. At that moment, a second explosion could boost the expansion, so that the next contraction is a little more violent. A properly timed pattern of explosions could feed a much larger resonance. Like repeatedly tapping a gong gently, you can build up a vibration. It's a very slow and small-amplitude vibration— on the order of centimeters—but one that poses difficulties for asteroid mining nonetheless.

There's a bit of confusion, by the way, over exactly why a two-kilometer-wide craft like the Near-Earth Asteroid Pulverizing Plant can't gobble up a resonating rubble pile just as easily as a stationary one. One look at NEAPP explains why: it is a gossamer construct, built to withstand incredible forces only with the finest margins.

"Oh, on that part I can assure you," Iino told me. "You don't design spacecraft with a large measure of structural overcapacity —it would be too expensive. NEAPP can't process a vibrating S38 because we hadn't thought to build it to deal with those kinds of forces orthogonal to the collecting structure. Why would we? We'll rectify that oversight with the next generation plant, you can bet on that."

So NEAPP clearly can't process S38. And S38 *is* resonating in exactly this way. Someone, or some thing, did that.

The simple explanation of Angavu as the causative agent, though, leaves much to be desired. For one thing, there's heat.

"I just don't buy it," said Kumiko Mazumdar, an asteroid researcher at the L5 Institute. "The whole argument depends on the rocks acting like billiard balls on a table—perfect elasticity. Yes, if they bounced off each other without losing momentum, even a tiny series of explosions could do the job. But rocks aren't elastic. When they collide, a lot of the energy gets translated into heat and friction. You lose too much energy to that heat to get such a resonance started."

Meaning?

"Meaning, all political questions aside, Nora Angavu couldn't have carried in a non-nuclear explosive device capable of doing the job. And she couldn't have gotten access to a nuke."

But a conglomerate could get access to a nuke?

I never got an answer for that one, because the Institute's lawyer cut in to end the interview. I was warned not to write that Professor Mazumdar was stating or implying that any specific corporations, agencies, or individuals other than Nora Angavu had perpetrated the sabotage of S38.

She wasn't; I understood that.

Surprisingly, Eli also bristles at the suggestion.

"That's a lie," he said. "Nora gave her life for something she believed in passionately, deeply. For something that a growing number of people believe in."

Chen helped me put that into perspective.

"Of course Eli said that," he said. "If this becomes a plot by the development industry to stick astro-environmentalists with a terrorist label, then his Madonna is unseated. But you have to admit, the incident did a lot of damage to relationships between a lot of people in the space community. I'm not saying any particular company could have been behind it—I don't think I believe it anyway. If you start to think in those terms, you wind up in some pretty Machiavellian neighborhoods."

But didn't Goldman tell Chen he'd seen a bomb?

Chen smiled. "Josh isn't exactly talking with any of us these days. So I can't ask him for you. But thinking back, right afterward, before the trial, I don't actually remember him saying he'd seen it; not in as many words. Remember, he was a biologist; he might not even have recognized a bomb if he did see it. I think maybe Lapinski saw it, and told him about it. God, that's going to get the corporate conspiracy theorists going, isn't it?"

Not everybody in the scientific community dismisses the possibility that a multi-munition carried in by Nora Angavu could have set S38 into gravitational resonance. Remember those microscopic glass spheres in the rubble pile's dust?

"It's an incredibly fine line," said Ingmar Ryall, an astrophysicist at the Lunar Advanced Research Laboratory. "But if you get it *just* right, those tiny ball bearings could change the picture significantly. I'm not saying that's how it happened; only that we can't completely rule it out. If Angavu did this, though, she was either a genius or incredibly lucky."

Ryall isn't sure about whether a micro-yield nuke could have been the culprit that started the resonance. It undoubtedly could impart enough energy to do the job, he said, but there's no trace of the radioactivity a run-of-the-mill device would have generated. There *are* specialized devices designed to yield less radiation, and by necessity we are measuring it through a lot of rock—nobody's getting near the core of this asteroid for some time to come. But that, again, leads inevitably to the conclusion that people in surprisingly high places must have supplied the bomb. And to the corporate conspiracy scenario.

I saved this question for last in my talk with Iino.

"This interview is over," he said simply. For what it's worth, he seemed offended to me—not defensive.

In the end, I think resonance is the only word that explains what did—or didn't—happen in the bowels of S38. Selfish or selfless; naive or wise; terrorist or martyr: whatever one says of Nora Angavu, she was a woman of powerful personality. We know how strongly that personality resonated in Joshua Goldman; we suspect, without knowing, that it may have resonated in Madeleine Lapinski.

Or perhaps it wasn't Angavu at all. Perhaps it had more to do with the religion she espoused—the idea of keeping wild things wild that so resonates with some people, and so infuriates others.

Fury is a kind of resonance, too.

In the end, we are left with two facts: Nora Angavu is dead, and in the coldness of space, a rubble-pile asteroid vibrates in resonance with her passage. I intend neither to lionize the woman nor to vilify her. Her passage, and the resonance it left behind, speak for themselves.

Perhaps it is up to you to decide.

THE PLANETOID OF DOOM: A RORY RAMMER, SPACE MARSHAL ADVENTURE

RON N. BUTLER

Space Marshal Rory Rammer stepped out onto the landing in front of the Space Marshals office for the City of Ceres. Watching the traffic flying past him on the Emshwiller Expressway, he waited for a break in the flow. When one opened up, he flung himself into the air.

Grabbing a u-bar on the nearest traffic stanchion, he pivoted through ninety degrees and settled into the stream of hurtling human bodies. An experienced zero-gee commuter, he flew freely, only touching a hand to the towline when he needed to change direction or avoid a collision. Behind him, the sunshine glow from the Expressway's origin at Ceres Central Park rapidly faded. Ahead, the flyway terminated at Ceres' South Pole and the pressure-docks for the big spaceliners.

Before he reached the tourist docks, though, he swung out of the river of humanity and onto the Conklin Crosstube. This took him toward the less-fashionable docks where lesser spacecraft and government rockets berthed.

Slowing to flash his ID at the guard shack, he bounced over a mechanic tucking into his lunchtime *bento* in an inopportune location, pivoted around a stanchion and shot down the center of the flexible tube connecting the Space Marshals rocketship *Silver Star* to Ceres' municipal pressure zone. Once through the open airlock, he caught himself against the catwalk running along the spaceship's long axis and began hand-over-handing 'up' to the rocket's nose.

"Skip!" he called ahead to the younger man sitting in the flight deck's right-hand acceleration couch. "Let's get the flight deck cleaned up. We've got a passenger along on this—" Then he caught the headrest of his own couch with both hands, bringing his zero-gee flight to an abrupt stop. In the couch lay a —thing.

Rammer frowned. "Skip? Why is there a big gumball machine in my seat?"

Cadet 'Skip' Sagan's eyes swung from his superior officer's face to the offending mechanism. In an aggrieved tone, he said, "He's not really a gumball machine, Rory."

In truth, the 'gumball machine' description applied best to the thing's 'head': A transparent globe a foot across, but filled with a variety of arcane sensors, not gumballs. Below that, a cylindrical body flared out at its base. A pair of tentacular arms sprouted from its sides, ending in four-fingered manipulators.

It talked, too. "Hi!" the thing said, some hidden speaker emitting a voice suitable for the sort of relentlessly cheery anthropomorphic rodent that infests Saturday morning vidcast shows.

A dirty suspicion began forming in Rammer's mind, having to do with the Commandant's unusually jolly mood when the marshal had left his office ten minutes before. "The Commandant said we'd be taking along a local officer—a 'Darryl Tate'— on this mission."

"That's me!" the machine chirped. "DARIL-T-Eight! 'Deep-Space Automated Remote Intelligence and Legal Telepresence, Model 8'! Please call me 'Daril'!"

"I'm going to have a long talk with the Chief Psychologist about the Commandant's sense of humor," Rammer muttered.

Sagan showed no sign he had noticed the marshal's sour mood. "He's a deep-space robot police officer, Rory. And a heckuva nice guy. We've been having the best time!"

"He's still in my seat."

"Oops!" Daril said. "I am sorry. Let me get out of the way." Fans hummed in its base and air-jets propelled the robot up from the couch until it hovered just short of the overhead console.

"Thank. You," Rammer growled.

"You're welcome! I won't require an acceleration couch, of course. Just strap me to the aft bulkhead when we're ready to boost and I'll be fine!" To demonstrate this, the little robot hummed over the crew's heads and somersaulted to float in midair, halfway to the bulkhead.

"Never any big nails around when you need 'em," the marshal muttered. "OK, 'Daril,' the Commandant said you'd fill us in on the background for our mission."

"Happy to! Ahem. Per Order Eighty-Five-Gee-Zero-Nine-Five-Special, Rocket Ship *Silver Star* and assigned crew plus special equipment DARIL-T-8, serial number—"

Rammer cut short the robot's recitation. "Skip it."

"—will proceed to asteroid Minerva Beta-Prime, catalog number—"

"Skip it."

"—to investigate shipments of suspicious materiel to the Heart of Gold Space Mining Company, Anson McGuire, Proprietor."

Suspicious materials? A drug case? Rammer wondered. *Munitions?* Not much market for either, out in the thin edge of the Asteroid Belt. "What sort of suspicious material?"

"Two metric tons of lithium deuteride."

Sagan looked as puzzled as Rammer felt. "Lithium

deuteride? What would anyone want with two tons of lithium deuteride?"

"Nothing springs to my mind," Rammer said. "Ask the parking meter."

"The—? Oh!" Sagan turned to face the robot. "Daril? What could you do with two tons of lithium doot?"

"Construct a hydrogen-fusion device!"

Despite his irritation, Rammer had to laugh and, if anything, his cadet enjoyed the joke even more. The marshal wiped an eye and asked, "What would an asteroid miner want with an H-bomb?"

"See, Rory?" Skip said. "I told you Daril has a great sense of humor."

"But I'm serious!" The machine actually sounded plaintive, its sensors whirring as it scanned the men's faces in turn.

"Yeah, right. C'mon, Skip, let's get strapped down. Those of us who require straps, that is. It's a long way to Minerva Beta-Prime."

The mechanical officer whirred aft, looking somehow dejected, and spread-eagled itself against the bulkhead. It did not speak again for the rest of the trip.

"Fifty feet per second. Thirty."

Rammer juggled *Silver Star*'s yoke to keep his guide stars centered in the coelostat while his right hand hovered over the ENGINE CUTOFF switch. In the other seat, Cadet Sagan called off relative velocity as the rocketship backed toward its target, a point in space offset from the asteroid Minerva Beta-Prime.

"Ten. Zero!"

The heel of Rammer's hand banged on the switch and the rumble of the main drive tapered off. The groaning and banging of cooling rocket motor nozzles replaced the rumbling and faded in turn. The marshal pulled his face back from the coelostat's rubber eyepiece and massaged his eyes. "Welcome to Minerva. Now, what are all these blue plastic drums floating around? I think we vaporized a couple of them with the drive exhaust. Skip, zoom in the video and see if you can read anything."

Sagan twiddled a zoom knob by the aft-facing video screen. One of the blue containers, spinning almost imperceptibly, loomed close enough to read its shipping label. "Got one, Rory. 'Denemore Chemical and Atomic, Inc. Lithium Deuteride, Commodity Grade.'"

Rammer stopped rubbing his forehead and leaned in toward the screen. "So McGuire really ordered two tons of lithium doot. Next question: What's he doing with it? Besides creating a hazard to astrogation."

Before anyone could speculate further, a querulous voice crackled over the open comm channel. "Ahoy the ship! Rocketship, identify yourself!"

The marshal keyed a mike. "This is the Space Marshals cruiser *Silver Star*, R. Rammer commanding. ID yourself."

The voice on the other end of the link did not sound impressed. "I'm Mackie McGuire. President, CEO and sole employee, Heart of Gold Space Mining. Now, what're you Feds doing sniffing around my claim?"

Sagan panned the video frantically over the slowly-rotating asteroid's rocky, red-brown surface. Apart from a dozen fresh-looking craters and a framework crammed full of blue drums at the South Pole, there was no sign of human activity.

"Mr. McGuire, where are you? I don't see a ship or an airdome."

The voice on the radio cackled. "I'm in my ship, the *Tarrier*, on t'other side of Minerva *Alpha*-Prime. That's this other chunk of rock about a hundred klicks Sunward. Here's my beacon."

A point of green light appeared on the radar display in the center of their instrument panel and began to blink steadily.

"Better hotfoot it on over! McGuire out."

Rammer replaced the microphone in its clip, a bit harder than strictly necessary. "OK, Skip, yaw the *Star* around. If McGuire won't come to us, we'll go to McGuire. And one other thing."

Sagan's hand paused in midair, halfway to the attitude controller. "Yeah, Rory?"

"Try not to hit any of his trash," Rammer growled.

Tarrier proved to be a battered *Hanshaw*-class mining tug, loosely tethered to the Sunward side of Minerva Alpha-Prime. McGuire apparently lived in his ship. No airdome habitat could be seen, though a miscellany of mining equipment—sunsails, spider-webbing, a magazine for explosive charges—covered most of the Sunward side. Rammer maneuvered the *Silver Star* to cut off any escape trajectory for the other rocket, and set the autopilot on "Station-Keeping." Then he and the cadet suited up and jetted over to *Tarrier*'s airlock.

Oh. And Daril, too.

Rammer cycled the tug's airlock and 'stepped' into the cabin, showing his badge in his right hand and an empty left hand. Drifting left to make room for his cadet to enter, he introduced himself and Sagan. That done, he batted away a drifting paper napkin (used) and wrinkled his nose at the thick fug of the habitat's air. It smelled as if McGuire had not vented his living volume to vacuum as a sanitary measure in a long time. The marshal had just finished re-stowing the badge when he heard the 'lock cycle a third time. *Oh, yeah*, he thought. *The robot.*

"Hi, there!" Daril squeaked. It surprised the marshal to see the machine show a badge of its own, attached to a little arm that extended from its fuselage.

Does the commandant let it arrest people? Rammer wondered. *Actual people?*

McGuire, in person, was a stocky man in his fifties, dressed in a patched spacesuit liner. He had the bare feet and nimble toes of a habitual zero-gee dweller; and Rammer suspected he styled his hair and beard by jamming his suit's helmet down over his head and trimming off whatever stuck out. Unlike most of the rock miners the marshal had met (semi-hermits by necessity), McGuire seemed delighted to have visitors and was distinctly talkative. Almost giddy, in fact. "Where'd ya get a talking gasoline pump?" he asked.

"A talking—" Rammer didn't follow.

McGuire covered a little smile with his hand, as if enjoying a private joke. "Watch this. Hey, you! Mr. Machine. Take your left manipulator."

The robot cheerily played along. "OK!"

"Now extend the first digit." McGuire demonstrated what he wanted with his own hand.

A faint whir was audible as the robot complied. "Sure! Like this?"

"Perfect. Now stick it in the audio pickup on the left side of your head-assembly." Metal met sensor with a distinct "Tink!"

"Hmm. He does look a bit like a gas pump," Rammer admitted. "Now, Mr. McGuire—"

"Call me 'Mackie.' Everybody does. Well, everybody does when there's someone around to call me anything at all. Which is every coupla years."

"OK, 'Mackie.' This is just a friendly Federal fact-finding visit. Did you recently take delivery of two metric tons of lithium deuteride?"

The question didn't appear to faze the prospector. If anything, it intensified the mischievous "I've-got-a-secret" vibe he gave off. "Yep. What about it? Doot's legal."

"So's cream cheese, but if you order two tons of it, people will talk."

"Heh! Guess so. Well, it's like this. Didja see Minerva Beta on the way in?" McGuire gestured vaguely in the direction of Capella.

"A typical nickel-iron asteroid, one thousand five-hundred eleven meters by three-hundred twelve meters," Daril threw in.

"Thank you for that no doubt accurate but totally irrelevant information, Daril," Rammer growled.

McGuire looked from the man to the machine, then shrugged. "Yeah. She's a good rock. High-grade cobalt, even some gold. But that nickel-iron's tough! I blow pits with these little atomic excavators—"

Rammer interrupted, "Beg pardon?"

"They're what I keep in that explosives storage module. Little pissant one-kiloton atom bombs to break up the ground. Then I sift through the rubble, refine out whatever's worthwhile, and drop it down to Mars or Earth on a sunsail."

The marshal nodded, uneasy. "I'm following you so far."

"But I got to thinking: Wouldn't it be a lot more efficient if I could move the whole asteroid down to Earth orbit?"

"We've moved asteroids before," Skip said. "You explode a series of atomic charges to nudge the asteroid from one orbit to another."

McGuire scoffed at such caution. "Yeah, but it takes forever. And a slewpot-full of charges. So I thought some more: What if I could move Minerva with just one, big charge? And that's where the doot came in!"

"I don't like the sound of this," Rammer said.

McGuire charged on. "If y' pack lithium deuteride around

an atomic fission exploder and set it off, when the fireball swallows the doot——"

"You get a fission-fusion reaction!" Skip threw in.

"And a really big bang!" McGuire finished.

"Of approximately fifty-seven point three megatons," Daril volunteered. "Assuming two tons of lithium deuteride, that is. An H-bomb. Hey, I was right!"

Rammer felt his second dirty suspicion of the day forming in his mind—and this one put his apprehensions about the Ceres commandant's sanity to shame. "McGuire, are you telling me you're actually doing this?"

"Well, yeah. But ya gotta set the charge off at just the right time to send the asteroid toward Earth."

Oh, Lord, thought Rammer. *Let that be tomorrow morning.* "Like when?"

McGuire grinned and glanced at an archaic wristwatch. "Like—right about now."

Enough light leaked around the edges of the sunshades over the ports and main windscreen on *Tarrier*'s bridge to turn the little space bright as a desert dawn. There was a sudden whispering against the hull of gas and dust blowing past.

"Hang on, boys! The shock wave'll be here in a sec! That's why I wanted you back here with me, behind Alpha."

The whispering swiftly increased to a hurricane-roar and *Tarrier* bucked and strained against its cables. Rammer heard his cadet yelling something about "von Karmann vortices," "a transient-flow medium" and "Reynolds numbers," but mostly he grabbed a thrust member and hung on until the mining ship shuddered to stillness once again.

McGuire recovered first. Of all of them, he had had the best notion of what was coming but even he seemed surprised by the violence of the shock wave. The air of the bridge was full of drifting manuals, pieces of clothing, fragments of mummified food and random trash. "Switch on the televideoscope there, youngster," he shouted to Sagan, "and we ought to be able to see Minerva Beta sailing away toward Earth."

The vid, suffering from a case of electromagnetic-pulse hang-over, took its own time coming up. When it did, it showed an enormous yellow-white fireball against black space, darkened with cloud-drifts of vaporized iron and nickel cooling into red-glowing dust-droplets and clinkers. It was a breath-taking vision, but it did not include the asteroid Minerva Beta-Prime.

The marshal found his voice first. "McGuire, didn't it occur to you that an asteroid might have flaws and cracks in it, places where it would split if you hit it hard enough?"

McGuire did not shift his eyes from the screen and Rammer could hardly hear his whispered response. "No."

Rammer muttered a particularly radioactive curse under his breath. "Didn't you ever talk this cockamamie idea over with anyone?"

"'Tain't no one out here to chin-wag with!"

"It's shattered into a million pieces!" said Skip, his eyes hot-bonded to the screen.

"Approximately three hundred thousand pieces between ten centimeters and two hundred meters across," added Daril. "Of which some twenty thousand will strike Earth, killing everything on the planet with the possible exception of tube worms in the deep ocean trenches."

McGuire went deathly pale.

"You have got to believe that we have not heard the end of this," said Rammer.

———

The marshal vacuumed dust off the outside of his spacesuit as *Tarrier*'s airlock finished pressurizing, then hung up the vacuum-head and pushed the inner door open. McGuire had curled up in a fetal position in mid-air. His cadet was riffling through papers clipped to the mining ship's plotting table/dinner table/spare bed: McGuire's calculations and engineering sketches for his grand scheme to revolutionize asteroid mining. For a change, the robot was 1) quiet and 2) out of the way, by the aft pressure bulkhead.

Sagan looked up as the door clicked shut. "Rory, you're back! How's the *Star*?"

Rammer pulled off his helmet and shook his head, disgusted. "A piece of debris clobbered our main comm antenna. We're out of touch with Ceres, Mars, Earth. Everyone. It wouldn't even do any good to rig a big Yagi aerial. Local space is full of nickel-iron dust from McGuire's H-bomb. It could take days to dissipate. Or weeks."

McGuire moaned and tried to tuck his head even more tightly into his arms. Rammer grabbed a bare foot and tugged at it, setting the miner to slowly rotating.

"C'mon, McGuire, on your feet. Or at least quit curling up like that. We need to talk."

Speaking into his armpit muffled the miner's voice. "I've killed everyone on Earth!"

"Nonsense! You haven't killed anyone. Yet. The first asteroid fragments won't hit Earth for—"

Rammer looked over at Sagan for an estimate, but the robot was faster. "Fourteen months, three days, seven hours. Approximately."

"Uh—thanks. Now McGuire, there are four big chunks more than fifty meters across. Daril, how much sidewise kick do we need to give a fragment for it to miss Earth by, oh, twice the orbit of the Moon, say half a million miles?"

A red light on Daril's "chest" flickered briefly. "Four point three feet per second. Currently."

"That sounds do-able. Now how many atomic detonators do you have left, McGuire?"

McGuire looked up for the first time since he grasped the disaster he had caused. "Seven."

"That ought to do it. Skip and I will help you nudge those four into safe orbits before we head back for Ceres."

"But that leaves thousands of the boogers still headed for Earth!" McGuire wailed. "They're not as big, but they'll wipe the planet clean as a billiard ball!"

"Not necessarily. McGuire, I have a proposition for you," Rammer said. "I can't make any promises. I'm not a judge. But I think my word will carry some weight with the authorities."

Suspicion and hope fought across the miner's features. "What is it?"

Rammer snapped a lanyard to his helmet and began unfastening his pressure suit's gauntlets. "You take *Tarrier* and follow the meteor swarm down toward Earth. Catch up with each fragment, the heaviest ones first, and kick them sideways so they'll miss the planet. If you do fifty fragments a day, you'll have 'em all cleaned out before you reach Earth."

McGuire's face fell. "It's no use! How can I pick out which ones are dangerous? They all look alike!"

"To the naked human eye, yes." Rammer indulged himself in a dramatic pause. "To the robotic eye, no."

"Hi, there!" Daril's automated enthusiasm could not have contrasted more with McGuire's gloom.

The marshal gestured at the robot. "We'll leave Daril with you to point out which fragment to hit next."

The machine jetted up to McGuire's shoulder and rotated to face him. "Sounds like fun! Let's get started!"

McGuire rubbed his chin, releasing a few whiskers to drift around the cabin. "Eh. What's the alternative?"

Rammer had a persuasive answer ready. "Probably death by slow torture at the hands of the survivors of the human race."

Silence fell over the cabin, growing longer by the second. Rammer finally said, "Well?"

"I'm thinking it over," said McGuire. "I'm thinking it over."

On the flight deck of the Silver Star, Marshal Rammer and Cadet Sagan ran through the last items on the pre-acceleration checklist.

"Attitude gyros caged," the marshal read.

"Check," Sagan responded.

Rammer pulled his crash harness tight. "Main turbopump to speed."

Behind them, a mechanical wailing rose in pitch, then stabilized.

The cadet touched his stylus to the checklist item so that it tuned dark, then tugged at his own harness straps. "Check."

"Checklist complete." Rammer secured his clipboard to a magplate and reached for the microphone switch. "Let's say our farewells. Rammer to McGuire. We're about to boost for Ceres. How about a progress report?"

On the radio, the robot's voice sounded little different than it did in person, but something very like exasperation had replaced its habitual enthusiasm. "No, no! Move the charge five centimeters down and eight right. Otherwise the fragment will spin."

McGuire, on the other hand, sounded tinny over a helmet mike. Especially when he was shouting. "'Five centimeters!' 'Eight centimeters!' You metal slavedriver, I was drifting rocks by hand before you were weaned off D-size batteries!"

"Nonetheless, it will spin."

I never knew there as a speech algorithm for 'snit,' Rammer mused. "Gentle—uh—'men.'"

"Huh? Oh. We're getting it done, Marshal." McGuire's sullen tone undercut his reassuring words.

"But we have fallen behind my work-progress projections." Daril's voder clipped its syllables a bit more tightly even than usual. "For reasons I will not go into."

"Say, Marshal, what would happen if we didn't get quite *all* these meteors deflected? Who would know?" McGuire paused just a second before going on. "Hypothetically, that is."

"I'm sure the Department of Science will train telescopes on the meteor swarm," Rammer said. "And if the fragments stop being deflected, likely they'll call in the Space Force."

"The-the Space Force?" McGuire didn't quite gulp.

The guys you call when it absolutely, positively has to be bombed until the rubble bounces, Rammer thought. He continued, "Who will probably lob in a salvo of big H-bombs—gigaton class—to vaporize the whole swarm."

"Gig-gigatons?"

"And anyone who happens to be too close," Rammer finished.

McGuire's laugh tried to be ingratiating. "Guess we'd better get crackin' on this boulder. Right, Marshal?"

"Right, Mackie. Rammer out."

Rammer turned to his cadet and saw the worry on the younger man's face. "Gee, Rory, you don't think the Space Force would really vaporize them, do you?"

"Might. Might not." The marshal could not resist a less-than-professional impulse. He leaned toward the younger man and stage-whispered, "Want to put a little money down on it?"

Sagan's shocked expression made it all worthwhile.

RUMBLINGS

ROY GRAY

BONNER / 1077 / LZP / 42

BEGINS

The situation underlying the urgency to progress Bonner can be summarised as follows:

• The technical problems of Bonner extractions are resolved but ethical dilemmas prevent implementation.

• A political settlement is necessary to obtain agreement from the naturals and gengineered polity.

• Galactic rotation and Hubble expansion limit access to planetary history beyond a depth of 500 years. In effect earlier pEarths are as remote as the stars and technology cannot provide an answer to the quandary.

• 50 years is the forecast time to Environmental Singularity, ecological transfusions need 30 years to be effective.

One means of countering ethical objections utilises catastrophic events with universal (multicontinua) dimensions. The augmented and artificial intelligence moieties agreed that taking advantage of past natural disasters (not human mediated catastrophes, such as wars) was acceptable; this remains controversial with the naturals.

Programmes of historical and archaeological research were instituted to look for evidence that our successor equivalents in parallel continua overcame such objections and performed extractions in our past. As a result of this work the following was retrieved, and decrypted, by Bonner researchers from electronic records dated as shown. The file is believed to be a diary and all dates were linked to a, now lost, daily events and news log. Similar log archives were in existence elsewhere and their records are now accessible but, to avoid questions of authenticity, no automatic links were established. Means to establish such links have been instituted for researchers keen to explore this aspect of the Late American Democratic Age in greater depth.

The excerpts below were considered pertinent to the Bonner Project and the naturals' expressed anxieties concerning the ethics of paratemporal operations. The author wrote very little on the relevant subject, though it was evidently an increasing concern to him from 2024 onward. Researchers added information [in brackets] as an aid to clarity but these are, as yet, unaudited. Bonner resource comments on the text remain in bold throughout.

From the diaries of L Z Palmer (1988 – 2032)

16/June/24, dark again today and still only 3°C at noon. Bring back global warming! Anniversary of food rationing today. Black-market [illegal/unofficial] coffee still costs more than coke. I also found some marmalade, an expensive import from England by the looks, you can never be sure these days, but a nice reminder of home.

Another internet crash so I used Berkeley [University Campus?] library to check geophysics of proposed refugee camp sites.

Met Joel. [J F Dobbs – Astronomer, 1990 – 2032] Astronomy still impossible for dust levels - and funding I expect. He worked on Spaceguard **[a 21ˢᵗ-century study of asteroids known as near-Earth objects ("NEOs") presenting an impact hazard because their orbits intersect Earth's]** as a post-grad and on airborne particles and settling rates since 2023 impact. Results very unpromising and he forecast another long dark winter.

Asked Joel's opinion of the 300 ms [millisecond] pre-impact seismic trace. Joel thought it looked like a coincident earthquake, the crust rose just prior to the moment of impact. Joel dismissed tidal effects because, at 0 - 300 ms [i.e. 300 ms prior to impact], NEO was about two mile [1 mile = 1.63 km] up and a mile down range and too small to start a quake by its own gravity. **[This is the first indication that our timeline may include an extraction. Other than Palmer there is no mention in any other records traced to date. This impact data has not been recovered. Its loss was assumed a result of the 2032 event.]** I had already discounted his suggestions after looking at traces from other instruments at different distances from the crater. It wasn't seismic wave dispersion effects, instru-mental errors caused by electrical interference from the atmos-pheric entry plasma or even a near miss shockwave from an unknown satellite of NEO. Couldn't convince Joel that NEO's arrival and this simultaneous quake were no coincidence but my explanation, a tidal effect, was obviously wrong.

Joel said if the mass was that wrong there'd be no South America left and the entire South from Frisco to Charleston would be suffering more than just minor quakes, dark days and brass monkey weather [unexplained phrase] in June.

I don't believe in coincidence.

Joel thought I should publish because, once the web is back to its normal reliability, word will get around, someone will see it and come up with an explanation. I said my letter to 'Geology' [Journal published by The Geological Society of America] was nearly ready to go. **[No report or letter was found in any extant archive.]**

25/June/24, 30 mins sunshine in Oregon, 5°C at noon, LA, today.

Brought bread on black market today. Mandarin characters, no English or Spanish, on the wrapping. It could be local, I suppose. Tasted fine.

More net problems, Berkeley again, met Maria Lopez. [M Lopez – Economist, 1980 - 2032] She led the team that completed the comprehensive ecological survey for the Brazilian Government. She was finishing her report when NEO impact took out the core of the surveyed area. That region, a major unspoiled area of rainforest, was due to be opened for development in 2023. Another coincidence?

'Took out' interesting phase. Why did I write that rather than 'obliterated'? I watched an old film last night in which people of the future, who can no longer reproduce, steal fertile people from the past under cover of accidents like air crashes. [Possibly 'Millenium' - 1989] Am I influenced by that idea? Could the seismic traces indicate someone stole the rainforest away under cover of the impact? Madness?

[A clear reference to the possibility of extractions]

28/June/24, darkness at noon, at least the big crowd kept the church almost warm. Sermon on cause & effect with plenty of references to Sodom and Gomorrah. Glad I never left the closet.

Our, suddenly fundamentalist, preacher suggested that the rain of fire followed from our recent, less than impeccable, earthly behaviour. I tend to dismiss this automatically. Why should God worry about what I think about doing in the privacy of my own home? But suppose our behaviour is upsetting someone, or something? Not our personal but our overall behaviour, like our effect on the planet, upsets us and maybe our descendants, or inheritors. Did I see evidence of an earthquake just before NEO impact or the results of millions of tons of the earth's crust, and its accompanying biosphere, being hijacked to the future? So was NEO an accident, where someone - or something - took advantage, or deliberate in order to take advantage?

[Clearly Palmer wonders if 2023 impact was not a chance event but engineered for an extraction, an analysis that surprised Bonner archaeologists.]

4/Sept/25, Refugees still pouring in, since the 'Mexicans' bombed the Trump Wall, and more camps required. Will keep me busy. Bitter arguments over sites because few want them as neighbours. Offered bribe to falsify results on proposed Palm Springs campsite. Very subtle, could not prove anything. Will say nothing. Can avoid problem by taking up offer of fieldwork. A survey of NEO crater is planned for next year. Never sent letter to Geology. Would put my reputation at stake. Weasely [compare 'weasel words' – common expression for avoiding dispute by moderating voiced opinion] but I don't have to mention my speculations so why draw attention to myself? If NEO was deliberate then these could be powerful people (?) to upset. If it wasn't the crater survey may provide answers.

[It is considered that Palmer's wariness and the

**lack of a published record is explained by his igno-
rance of the limits to paratemporal translations.]**

14/Sept/25, Leg infection is antibiotic resistant. Choice is more treatment or a tin leg, which I'll probably still need after the treatment. Just bad luck. I didn't even catch the bug when I fell. Acquired in hospital, in Brazil or here. DNA evidence suggests here most likely. Apparently I can sue. Tin leg, prostheses as medics say, are pretty good. I'll go for that option. Fall for nothing, as I might say, since I went to Brazil for evidence, found nothing either way **[no evidence of a Bonner extraction?]** and fell trying to rescue a crashed drone from NEO crater. Invited to write a book about NEO impact and effects. This time it's not a bribe - publisher is Cranmore of New York. Popular science covering astronomy, geology, geophysics and atmospheric physics. Joel, who is now a weatherman on Calweb, would be ideal as co-author. I want 'NEO, Two Years On' as title. Cranmore want 'WHOMP!' Offered more work on refugee camps, not fieldwork though.

15/Dec/25 Coffee off rations, still scarce but cheaper than cocaine now, apparently. Saw Joel about book. He is happy to do the astronomy and atmospheric effects. We settled on 'WHOMP! NEO Two Years On' as the title. Embarrassing but we had to give Cranmore a half win. Joel asked about my pre-impact seismic mystery and if it was going in the book. I'd forgotten I'd told him so I had to say something. He was scathing about the idea said it would be like someone going back in time to kill their grandmother. I did point out that he was assuming that our successors will be human. He countered that the millions of years required to evolve any non-human successors will give the biosphere plenty of time to recover from humanity's depredations and it's much easier to assume any time travellers are our descendants.

I asked if that meant he believed some of this but he would only concede 'putative time-travellers' for the sake of argument; plus extraordinary claims need extraordinary evidence. I don't have that and he's probably right. I do feel better for talking about it. I had no intention of including anything about time travel in the book. Joel joked we might outsell Von Daniken if we did. [E Von Daniken – speculative-history author]

15/May/28. Why do they keep building refugee camps in earthquake zones? To make sure they can't settle down is the rumour, but in reality because no one else wants to live there. Also there are more planned for Republican [A political allegiance] areas since 2024. Most refugees now from south of the strike but at least the numbers are down by two million in the past year. Even so Brenman [E Brenman - US Commissioner for Refugee Affairs, 2024 – 2032] asked me to join a complete survey of Yellowstone to identify potential campsites. It'll be a huge survey, fauna, flora, geology and geography because the Sierra Club [a North American organisation committed to preservation of the natural environment] are insisting on full environmental-impact statements for any planned encroachment. I don't blame the Club for objecting but they won't win because nobody wants a camp in their back yard. Their local members weren't slow about objecting to the Menlo camp. I know I am/was piling a lot of fantastic premises on one observation and Joel sort of talked me out of it but this survey reminds me of Maria Lopez's Brazilian rainforest survey before NEO impact. There are some big volcanoes in Yellowstone.

[Clearly Palmer is concerned that supposed time travellers from his future may be able to influence political events in his era.]

7/June/31 Rationing ended, coffee is plentiful; as is cocaine I'm told. New tin leg fitted, nothing really wrong with the old one, but this is improved and more suited to fieldwork though Wyoming is more forgiving than the upper Amazon, or what's left of it. Met Jim Tellman [J Tellman – microbiologist 1979 - 2032] on survey team. Jim worked on biowarfare defense for DOD. Still consults for them but very little since NEO. Apparently the cholera outbreak at the Carmel Valley complex may not have been chance and poor hygiene. So Jim is looking at the potential for contamination of water resources because of the threats against refugees. Unbelievable!

More time to read with all the coming and going to Yellowstone. Joel sent me a book on time travel, 'Time Travel in Einstein's Universe' by Gott. [Probably 2022 Edition, J R Gott'] Much speculation that it is impossible to return to our own past but, if there are parallel universes, it might be possible to travel into their past. This avoids causality paradoxes like killing your grandmother. So if you are ruthless and/or desperate enough, you could raid the past of a parallel Earth without affecting your own history. **[Parallel continua were highly speculative science at this time but often featured in fiction.]** This idea might explain why and how the future, or a, future could restore its own biosphere. Hijack it from parallel worlds. Also resolved Joel's point about the millions of years required to evolve our successors. Artificial Intelligence has been predicted to take over from humanity in mere decades but why would an AI need to repair the biosphere?

So was NEO really an accident, or was it camouflage? If the latter why bother? Not much chance I'll ever have an answer.

Gott also described 'jinni', a type of time loop paradox. As an example, while building a time machine suppose I found a tennis ball. Assuming it had come through the window I pick it up and put it on a nearby shelf. Then I finish the machine and want to do a quick test to check it works. I look round and see the tennis ball and send it back 10 minutes in time. This is the moment where I found it. The ball is a jinni, it has no origin; it just loops through time.

My worry is something Gott called information jinn; ideas that loop through time. The worrying scenario: I see and interpret the NEO impact seismic traces and write about them in terms of a chunk of rainforest being removed under cover of an asteroid strike. This speculation is read in the future where someone/thing then decides to use the idea to replenish their biosphere. They alter the orbit of an asteroid in the past and bring about the disaster, so completing the loop. Thus my speculations lead to or are even part of such a jinni. There's little chance of my starting such a disastrous sequence, as Gott thinks the future could only dip into the past of a parallel universe, but why take the risk? I'll encrypt this diary and save it to a secure data haven in Australia.

[Multiplex continua symmetries ensure Palmer's concerns about jinn were baseless for downbranch translations]

13/July/31. Happy birthday me. 44 today, Ecard from Cranmore with note, total print sales were 37000. E books another 6000. Spanish edition, 12000 and 900. Won't be rich but not bad.

Riots in the Laguna camp last night. I take some pride in the fact that it survived the 6.9 quake pretty well with very few casualties but the residents weren't quite so sanguine. Rumblings in Yellowstone at very low intensity. Helium^4 reading raised. Is this the first sign or is my imagination running wild? USGS [United States Geological Survey] were reluctant but now I can do more fieldwork I'll move into Fishing Bridge. The RV Park is commandeered as survey HQ. Signed insurance release against employer liability because of tin leg. If my suspicions are correct I could be in the right place if the park is taken and so accompany it to the stratosphere or to its destiny on a future Earth. If it is the latter, wherever or whenever that might be, I may have a nasty surprise for them. Presuming they are human, especially far future human, their immunity to cholera may be less than perfect.

11/April/32 More helium and rumblings but still low Richter. Passenger flights to the southern hemisphere are fully re-established now so I can stay here, and check out my theory, or move somewhere safe, like Australia. The survey is complete and we have to provide the final report in September. Tellman is coming tomorrow so I'll try to persuade him to get me some samples. If he can I'll stay.

Hollywood output back to 2022 levels. Everyone says things are back to pre NEO normality. The refugee influx has been good for business with DOW [A stock-market index based on share prices] back at 30K. I'm wealthy, though it's very volatile wealth.

17/July/32 There is still a black market for coffee and chocolate in Wyoming. No rationing but there are shortages and the local laws prevent regular shops from raising prices. Despite tin leg I can ride a mountain bike quite well. I'll get another and some spares. A spare tin leg could be a wise investment as well so I've ordered two. Tilt, gravimeter, helium[4] and seismic surveys in Yellowstone look somewhat ominous to me but nobody else is concerned. The change is small but I think it significant. Normal variation according to the YVO [Yellowstone Volcano Observatory] but this is slow and steady. Even Baxter [J D Baxter – Volcanologist 1993 – 2032] at NY thought I was over reacting but he said he would come over in August. Tellman works with ebola now for DOD; I wonder if I can persuade him? I'd have to tell the whole story and might get the same reception from him that I got from Joel. If the gravimetric evidence strengthens I'll risk it.

8/Aug/32 My section of the survey report is now complete and I'm back to campsite geology again from next week. Preparations are continuing, assuming approval next year, according to Brenman's office.

I think it will happen. Tellman is here tomorrow. I'll have a word. Need to make some preparations beyond the shooting practise. At least I'm scoring a consistent 70% now. YVO more concerned about eruption. Records show similar readings in the past but not so sustained and steady. We've been told to keep quiet to avoid panic while Washington thinks about it but some are preparing reasons to move their families to the east coast.

Whatever Tellman decides this time I'll be there, waiting. I'll stay in the RV for now and camp out to be on site when it blows. I think I'll get a dog but not sure which type. Not too big because of feeding problems and park regulations on dogs. Can't say how long it will be before they won't matter any more. It will be interesting to see the future, or should I say a future, if my fears are well founded. If not, and the worst happens, then it will be quick, for all of us. Bought some guns and ammo and stashed stores, tents, fuel, food, water, bikes, tin legs, spares etc. at strategic points, just in case. It would be interesting to see a new universe but not at the price we may have to pay.

17/Aug/32 Tellman came up trumps and I've been immunised. Have also got a satellite phone so I can maintain an audio link direct to the data haven, until the very last possible minute, should the worst happen. My dogs will be here tomorrow. They will be six weeks old then. I should have got them earlier really but I may have more time than I thought. Must get dog food reserves in place. Pity I never learnt to ride. [Equines?]

22/Sept/32 Government evacuating everyone within 100 miles of Yellowstone. I've been consulted on sites to set up drones, extra cameras and instruments to watch the volcano and monitor any eruption. We start that tomorrow. Passive and active radio tags will enable them to be found if they are covered in ash. Can't see me flying any drones but others will. I'll snaffle some tags and buy a transmitter/receiver myself. They sound useful if you need to find things, or people, that are lost or buried. I'll keep a tag if they find me or my body it will prove my theory is madness. If they don't it won't prove anything, as hot lava rarely leaves much to be found.

25/Sept/32 Controversy over evacuation area in Sunday's news. Many are saying it's too little. CNN [a broadcast news organisation] asked me for my opinion so said I thought it was OK. Lies but it's hardly possible to evacuate the entire Mid West and I could be wrong.

10/Oct/32 **Transcript of audio data. Much of this data is irrelevant to Bonner, examples being the times when Palmer is talking to one, or both, of the dogs. Only data that seems to bear on the project is included here but has not been audited and the signal was very noisy. Here text in parenthesis is interpolated from context, natural human insight and/or signal processing. The remaining data is <u>available</u> to those wishing to check our judgement or re-evaluate the complete file.**

16:25 "Looks like the entire existing crater and lake are the hottest seats in the house, so I think I'm in the right place, on the lakeshore halfway between Fishing Bridge and Old Faithful."

16:27 "We're really [shaking?] now, I've got the dogs tied, they're really terrified. So am I."

16:28 "Noise deafening. No internet now and no idea what the phone [is] sending. I'm shouting but can hardly hear myself. There are huge clouds of dust. Drones and planes can't fly in this. Tin leg dislikes the vibration, so do I."

16:29 "We installed IR [Infra red] cameras to see through the dust so why didn't I bring IR night-vision kit? Because I'm stupid."

16:30 "Low rumble, getting louder like a train approaching. Fell for the third time, ground movement very violent now. No sign of time machines or [you/your/new? efforts/effects? flows?] yet."

16:32 "Can't get a [return signal?] and [unsure this is getting through?] Visibility [very?] poor and the sky is [full of?] ash and [dust/dark?]. Oh my God..." **No further data.**

No further relevant entries were discovered and there is no record that Palmer's body was found. This diary is the only indication that NEO 2023 Impact and Yellowstone 2032 were not natural events. Palmer does not provide unequivocal evidence of extracontinua interference but he raised sufficient doubt to persuade many waverers that we are, or were, victims. Continua spread indices for NEO impact and Yellowstone, now in preparation, will provide statistical evidence that natural processes caused those events, or otherwise.

Palmer's work also prompted a review of the project's modus operandi and supported the improved security, covert approach since adopted for all extracontinua operations.

Palmer's deductions will probably be replicated in adjacent continua and his musings on the use of ancient diseases suggests that further precautions are warranted following a Bonner extraction.

The judgement was not unanimous. The one dissenting opinion, Quandell, is that we may be entering an unusual form of jinni, which passes across the fan of parallel continua, stepping one continuum per cycle. This 'dislocation' jinni will persist until one continuum breaks the cycle.

It was agreed that the search for a parallel Earth with a sophont free, pristine biosphere would be maintained until Bonner implementation is irrevocable. Overall our committee is in no doubt that the ethical concerns will now be overcome and the Palmer file has provided the final justification for Bonner implementation.

Bonner/1077/LZP/42

ENDS

BAD EGG: A SUNDOG TALE

BRUCE F. WEBSTER

JACE BANSSON, captain-by-inheritance of the star trader Sundog, rotated his head to examine the synthesized view his ship projected in a surrounding hemisphere.

"Well, this isn't good."

Hundreds of other spacecraft were rising from fields on Rwatha's surface for scores of miles around; at least half were somehow being destroyed before making it out of atmosphere. Bright bursts, puffs of smoke, and occasionally visible falling debris marked each ship's demise. Ships staying in atmosphere and trying to flee over the horizon were likewise being shot down.

Superimposed on the view, nearly overhead, was a bright red speck with a projected course and arrival time. This tracked a not-very-small asteroid, about three klicks wide, on which someone had mounted quite a few sub-c engines before aiming it at Rwatha and accelerating it to a tiny but measurable (and still growing) fraction of lightspeed.

Jace smiled a thin, bitter smile. "And I didn't even get the eggs."

The trip to Rwatha had appeared to be straightforward. The native race, the Whutta (singular: W'at), had a reproductive cycle that produced pre-emergent larva in solid casings: eggs. But each batch included a few infertile eggs that held near-priceless complete organics with a multitude of uses. The colony of Frasgird needed one such egg.

And what Frasgird needed, Jace had to get for them. A few years ago, Jace had been pulled out of the glass mines of Wadti, where he'd been enrolled in a "family debt repayment arrangement" that was effectively long-term slavery. His uncle Brock had been robbed and murdered, leaving Jace the Sundog, few other assets, and a massive contractual obligation: delivering crucial goods to Frasgird, a new colony founded to pull the fractured, scattered, and dwindling human race back from inevitable extinction.

If he could fulfill the contract with Frasgird, he would be free of the glass mines forever. So Jace had to become a trader-slash-smuggler himself: buying and selling to build up his own financial resources, then purchasing goods for the colony as funds permitted, all the while dodging pirates and assassins. The strain took its toll. Jace had been young when freed from the mines, was still young, but his face showed more age than his years. His dark, lean face had a weathered look that suggested sailing on open waters, not traversing the stars.

Getting the latest cargo for Frasgird should have been easy. But the Whutta proved nearly impossible to negotiate with, cheap and unyielding. And they only sold their eggs in complete batches, mostly fertile and a few infertile, at astronomical prices. Jace's only leverage was that each Whutta clan was fiercely competitive with all the others.

Jace had made multiple visits to the Rwatha trade exchange,

decked out in his finest trading outfits, and had spent hour after hour in bids and negotiations. He thought he was getting close to a deal, but had come back to the ship to sleep for the night.

However, this morning while in the dryshower, Jace had felt the subtle vibrations that meant the Sundog was underway.

"What's up?"

Sundog answered through the subvocal commlink in Jace's skull. =Get out and get dressed. Whutta is under attack.=

The shower door opened; Jace stepped out and began pulling clothes on. "What, the city?"

=The whole planet. Get up here.=

Jace got dressed and dashed for the pilotage.

Now securely braced and strapped in his captain's chair, Jace watched the destruction around him. Detection of the asteroid and its deliberate trajectory had triggered an effort by several of the Whutta regional covens to deflect or destroy the asteroid, which in turn revealed that forces were in place, both dirtside and on orbit, to prevent just that.

Presumably, that same party was the one blowing the fleeing ships—Whutta and otherwise—out of the sky.

Sundog, for its part, was now flying cross-country at high speed and low altitude, tracing a broad arc roughly 200 klicks in diameter and centered on the planet's cluster of spaceports. That seemed to be a safe course for now. Jace has asked the ship to opaque the floor and sidewalls after witnessing a few near-collisions with both artificial and natural structures.

Jace looked at the time-to-impact countdown and grimaced again. "Uh, do you have any hope of getting us out of here? We are on a bit of a deadline."

Sundog answered through the subvocal commlink in Jace's

skull. =Still analyzing the pattern of destruction. Some ships are in fact making it out of atmosphere and seem to be successfully leaving orbit as well.=

"Any idea how?"

=There is a hint of a common pattern among the broadcasts from the surviving ships. My best guess is that they either paid someone off or are in league with the beings doing the destroying, and they have a safe passage code interwoven with their transmissions.=

"Can you fake it?"

=Not yet.= Then: =Hold on.=

Jace frowned at the ship's unusual caution; then the projected view dimmed to near-black and Jace was slammed into the side of his chair in spite of the ship's inertial dampeners. "Hey! No rough stuff."

=Hush, child. We are trying to outrun a shockwave.=

"I'll 'child' you—and what shockwave?" Jace looked at the view again. "The rock's not due to impact for another hour or so."

=Someone set off an anti-matter bomb in the middle of the exodus; I do not know which party. But I am going to see if I can use the blast front to mask our escape beyond the safe perimeter. I hope it has disrupted whatever tracking and targeting system has been shooting down ships.=

"Clever alliteration. What if you're wrong?"

=Nice knowing you, Jace.=

"Thanks. Can you make the interior transparent, top to bottom?"

The ship's walls faded away, and Jace inhaled involuntarily as he found himself flying a hundred meters or so over a mix of settled and unsettled countryside at a speed that must have been close to one klick every few seconds. The ground beneath was a blur; Jace could only track buildings, fields, and surface features for a split second before they passed beneath. Dampeners masked the ground-hugging trajectory of the ship, but Jace felt dizzy and a touch nauseated anyway. He bent his knees and an enveloping chair formed beneath him; he closed his eyes and gave his stomach a minute or so to settle. He winced a bit as he imagined the shock wave they were leaving behind.

"I… I had no idea you could do this. Go this fast, this low, I mean."

=We go this fast all the time when we lift to orbit. But there, we are going more or less straight up through thinning atmosphere. The air is denser down here; I have our shields on in full battle mode and shaped to provide an aerodynamic shell. As such, we are burning through fuel faster than I would like. But we still exist, so I think we have escaped the killing field for now.=

Jace blinked as the ground beneath them turned into extensive grasslands. Clouds filled the horizon, then the sky, and then everything went gray and wet; Jace assumed they were flying through rainfall. He frowned at the thought of the windstorms they might be leaving in their wake, then realized that any sapes below had more important and inevitably fatal concerns.

I need to get a grip on myself.

Jace leaned back and raised his legs; the seat shaped him into a reclining position. He mentally set himself for a 20-minute nap and closed his eyes.

He opened his eyes to clear sky among white clouds. Sitting up, he saw they were maneuvering through mountain valleys, with patches of what looked to be blue-tinted snow on some of the slopes. "So, what's the effect of the impact going to be?"

=The planet itself will survive; most of the biosphere will not. The impact will transfer roughly two thousand yottajoules of energy to this planet in a brief period of time. The surface will be scoured and burned, seas will boil, and the atmosphere will ignite. Everything and everyone on the surface of Rwatha will likely perish.=

Jace looked outside as the ship raced down the far side of the mountain slopes towards more farmlands and then a few heartbeats later into open water stretching to the horizon. "So why don't we just lift and go?"

=I am not sure it is safe. I am in fact surprised that we still exist; that suggests the am-bomb was set off by a faction on this planet to destroy the ships that were successfully escaping. It disrupted the forces enforcing the blockade, but I am sure that they are positioned elsewhere in orbit around the planet, not just over the spaceport region.=

Jace watched the sea (ocean? very large lake?) screaming beneath the ship for a minute or two. Looking back, he could see the enormous plume of spray the ship left in its hypersonic passing. Occasional blinks of white and color suggested vessels on the water; the ship appeared to weave slightly to avoid them.

Jace looked ahead again, where he could see a thin edge of land growing rapidly out of the water's horizon. "So, what do we do?"

=We set down somewhere and wait for impact. We are far enough over the horizon to be blocked from the actual radiation burst as the rock punches through the atmosphere. Then we time our escape to coincide with the blast front coming over the horizon.=

Jace watched mountain peaks, some tipped with snow, appear on the horizon as land grew nearer. "The Whutta here on their world are all going to die, aren't they?"

=Yes, along with anyone else stuck here. Were the asteroid traveling at normal in-system speeds, even in an opposing orbit, it would not be big enough for a full-extinction impact. Coming it at three percent of light-speed is an entirely different story.=

Jace flinched slightly as the ship came off the water back over land and began terrain-hugging again. After a time of silence, he said, "Can we save anyone?"

=The best we could do is load some Whutta into one of the cargo bays, put them in stasis, and take them to another world. Pupate stage would be best; we could fit more in.=

Oh right. We still need to get some eggs for Frasgird.

=We do risk attack by those thinking they can seize and control this ship,= Sundog cautioned.

"How about an isolated group? On a farm or homestead or whatever it is that the Whutta do outside their cities."

The front view obscured and became a geographic map of what Jace assumed was the landmass just below them, a tiny neon blue image of the ship indicating their current location. Color-shaded regions appeared reflecting population distributions and densities, with blue strands indicating ground-based transits. A scattering of specs showed up in a highland region on the far side of the mountains towards which they were rapidly climbing; green circles outlined several.

=These are some candidate locations. I am contacting them now.=

Jace watched the countdown timer in silence for a minute or so.

=I have found a small collective that has pre-emergent pupae from several different families. That should give genetic diversity and allow the emergents to readily cross-breed. They ask, however, that we take one adult W'at along as well.=

"Can we pull that off?"

=Yes. They have made a most generous offer to buy the cargo from both pods, so that we can take more along.=

Jace frowned. "That doesn't sound right. I've spent the last few weeks arguing endlessly with Whutta over prices for cargo, fuel, repairs. Tight-fisted doesn't begin to describe them. Not that they have fists or even hands. But if they did, they'd be tightly clenched."

=They are in fact penurious.= Jace rolled his eyes; the ship seemed ever-intent on improving Jace's vocabulary. =On the other hand, we are talking about family and species survival. Also, word of our offer seems to have leaked out; I am receiving additional bids and pleas from homesteads in the region.=

"Yeah, but... I don't know." Jace looked down at the treetops and occasional grasslands racing below his feet. "Look... can we vanish somehow? Make it look as though we're still going toward those farms but actually stop somewhere well short?"

=I need you to pull a full line of components from the shields bay and dump them to the weapons bay, so I can build a missile with them.=

Jace started moving while the ship was still talking; the shield subsystem panel opened as he got there, and he started pulling out units. =We will launch the missile and simultaneously land,= Sundog continued. =The missile will put out a shield the same shape and size as our current settings.= Jace wheeled to the now-open weapons bay and placed the units inside, even as raw materials poured in and began shaping themselves. =The loss of shield strength will limit our low-atmosphere speed and leave us a bit more vulnerable to attacks.=

Jace went back to the pilotage and dropped back into the seat.

=I am ready to launch the decoy now. Where would you like me to land?=

"The closest small homestead that is not making any bids."

=Brace yourself. This is going to stress my inertial dampening systems a bit.=

Jace, having bitten his tongue more than once during fights with would-be pirates, clenched his mouth shut and threw his head back against his seat. The headrest snapped itself around his forehead and shoulders; the chair wrapped itself around his limbs and torso. A second or two later, he felt his body try to throw itself through the upper front portion of the pilotage as the ship instantly plunged to the grassland below and came to a stop under some trees. The seat released him, and Jace looked up to see that impact was due in a bit less than fifteen minutes.

"OK, where's the homestead?"

=Northwest, 1.2 klicks. I have detached the cargo pod but have transferred at least one energy weapon onto it. Be careful.=

Jace, again already moving, dashed back, and jumped into the pod's control chair. The front of the pod sealed behind him, and the pod began to back itself out from between the ship's nacelles. "Put me on a tight beam with the homestead, if you can get a connection."

=Done.=

Light! Salvation in death! Carry us from here! The chimes formed words in Jace's mind.

Jace opened his mouth and spoke; what he heard through his headset were chimes as well: *In despair, but for no gain, I offer room for three-thirteens of still-young and a nurturer.*

What do you offer us for this boon of glory?

Ah, these are the Whutta I know, Jace thought. *Hope I can shortcut the usual haggling.* Out loud: *I can scarce part with two-and-a-fraction-thirteens of a-grav units.*

Such a paltry sum for immortality! It is not enough!

Then I return to my ship now and flee the world-death. Or I can leave you four-and-a-median-thirteens of a-grav units.

Done! Done! Come quickly! Even as the unknown W'at assented, the cargo pod pushed through the vegetation canopy, and the homestead lay before him, an intricate complex of small towers linked by meter-wide pathways in upper/lower pairs held above the ground by slim poles. Jace focused on the open end of one pathway complex, and the pod swerved, pivoted, and backed itself up with the left cargo bay aligned properly. The bay door opened, and a-grav units began to feed onto the lower beltway, which carried them into the homestead complex.

As the last of the 60 a-grav packages left, the upper beltway lowered a bit and began to drop a stream of gleaming, brightly-decorated spheres about the size of Jace's head. Force-field manipulators caught each one and neatly placed it within the bay.

=Jace, the decoy is gone. I have lost all signals.=

"Any idea what happened?"

=Sorting through the data flood planetwide... looks like another anti-matter blast.=

"Uh, it wasn't in a designated ship zone, and there are no large population zones there. Why would anyone blast there? Were there any ships there other than our decoy?"

=Impossible to tell at this point. Curious, though. The most likely and yet least comfortable conclusion is that it was meant for us.=

"Well, hopefully the shooter thinks we're dead now."

Jace turned back to the cargo bay. As one layer of spheres was completed, a rigid net formed from the bay's walls, protecting the spheres below and forming a floor for the new ones coming in. As the last of the thirty-nine spheres was put into place, a slightly denser net formed in time to receive the Whutta nurturer.

The adult W'at came rolling off the pathway as an armor-plated sphere roughly a meter in diameter. As it was placed onto the receiving net, it unfolded into a flat, intricate shape about fifteen centimeters thick. Even as it did so, the pod began pulling away from the homestead's pathways and heading back for the ship. The left cargo bay sealed itself, and the quantum stasis indicator came on.

Go now! Gain your glory, while we perish with your meager offering! Tell us your lineage, that we may curse it as we burn!

Jace thought for a moment, then replied. *I have no lineage! I am a solitary orphan! My heritage dies with me! My name is Jace, Jace Alone!*

Shocked silence from the homestead, as if Jace had uttered an obscenity or blasphemy. *Perhaps I did.*

But then more chimes: *We adopt you! You are hereafter Jace ma Whre na Gat! Go and save your kin! Our legacy is yours! Take our accounts! We transmit our codes!*

Nearing the ship, Jace said to Sundog, "We may come out ahead after all. What's their balance like?"

=Checking… well, I suppose that is consistent at least. Their planetside accounts show a deficit.=

"How much?" The pod pulled back between the nacelles, docked itself, and opened its front.

=2941 credits.=

Jace sat down in the pilotage, felt restraints flow over most of his body. "Go ahead and pay it. We have at least that much in planetside accounts, don't we?"

=Yes, we do.=

"Not likely to be able to cash that out now. Might as well compound our good deeds." He thought for a second about Whutta culture, then added: "Pay a bit more—leave their account with a positive balance."

=Done.= A pause. =Mark: three minutes to impact. I am going to lift off and hover at a low altitude one minute before impact.=

"And then?"

=Then we try to outrun apocalypse.=

The ship maneuvered itself out from under the trees and into an open field, hovering a meter or so off the ground. After another minute or so, the ship said, =Receiving tight beam from the homestead again.=

Jace ma Whre na Gat! You accepted your legacy!

Jace smiled wryly, but mustered some enthusiasm as he chimed back, *Yes! With honor!*

Our physical lineage lives on! We die with profit! We micturate on our non-kin groups!

I rejoice with for my vanishing kin! Jace couldn't think of much more to say. *Have a happy last five minutes of existence?*

Rejoice for yourself as well! Still-young 13, 17, and 29 are yours! Do not examine until you reach another system!

Well, well, well. Frasgird will be happy. Out loud, Jace chimed, *I guard our legacy! Safe passage beyond!*

We burn and die, or die and burn. The rest is silence. Fly, you fools.

Jace stared at the view in front of him for several seconds. He had never heard Whutta chime without the inflection that he always mentally translated to an exclamation point. Plus, the last two phrases seemed to indicate that the Whutta on this farm knew—or at least suspected—that Jace was human.

The ship was now heading at slow speeds and low altitude down into a river valley. It moved over the middle of the river, then settled into the water, holding its position well above the bottom and against the current.

"Quick check. The ships that were being destroyed back in the landing zone—can you tell how many were carrying humans?"

=I have some data cached; I will see what more I can pull from the planetary nets. Given the current chaos, I may be able to tap into some feeds I would not otherwise. Two minutes to impact.=

The view before Jace changed to show a 3-D image of Rwatha scaled down enough to show the path and current location of the approaching speck, which moved at an unnerving rate of speed, covering roughly the diameter of Rwatha every second or two. "So, why didn't someone deflect or destroy the asteroid?"

=Notice that we are still stuck on the planet ourselves. Nobody on Rwatha—except for those behind the attack—knew about the asteroid until a few hours ago. Rwatha is not a high technology planet, nor a very military one—but even if it were both, no one would expect an asteroid in a well-mapped system to leave a stable orbit and shift to an intercept path with an inhabited planet—and especially not at a measurable fraction of lightspeed.= A pause. =One minute to impact.=

"Frak. Can't we just leave now?"

=It might be a very short trip. Someone set off that am-bomb right in the path of our decoy. Also, while my data so far is incomplete, I have not found a single ship with humans on board that has escaped atmosphere, whereas I have identified a significant number of ships with humans that were destroyed. Correlation probabilities have not reached a conclusive level, but the theory that someone is trying to kill humans on Rwatha seems viable. Whether that second anti-matter blast was aimed at us—if, in fact, it was aimed at us—just because you are human or for some more specific reason is beyond the data right now.=

Jace frowned. "We've only been here for about 100 hours—seven or so local days. Setting up this asteroid attack must have taken hundreds of days, maybe thousands. Us being here has to be a coincidence."

=Agreed. Unless, of course, it is not. In the meantime, move to the pilotage. I want to build up some layers of protection around you. This could be a difficult flight. Impact in ten seconds.=

Jace moved quickly to the pilotage as the ship lifted to just above the treetops and hovered there. He sank into the seat, with material flowing over his entire body, as well as into his ears, mouth, and nostrils. He felt his body relax and then fade away.

=Three. Two. One. Impact.=

Jace felt a profound, silent blow, as if every molecule of his being had been struck simultaneously with a nano-scale hammer. All light vanished.

He started to subvocalize and realized he couldn't speak, hear, or breathe.

He also realized that the ship was no longer in his brain.

Oh, frak.

He tried to lift his arms up. The material around them resisted, then started to give. Jace got his right hand up first and began to tear at the material on his face with it as he struggled to get his left hand free also. Within a few seconds, he was pulling material out of his mouth and nostrils with both hands. Once he could breathe, he started peeling it away from his eyes, ears, and the rest of his face.

He could still see nothing, though he could hear his own gasping. The ship appeared to be oriented at a strange angle. He continued to tear away at the material and work himself free of the seat. As he did so, light began to appear again, tiny glowing spots on the interior walls, largely clustered in one corner of the pilotage. In a matter of seconds, connecting lines of light grew between the spots, then spread out from there through the walls and surfaces, though entire portions of the pilotage remained dark.

The material surrounding Jace's legs suddenly withdrew back into the seat, and he grabbed an armrest to keep from falling out against a nearby bulkhead. The overall light in the pilotage came up, and information displays began to reform themselves.

"Ship, what the hell happened?"

"Reorganizing. Wait." Jace actually jumped a bit to hear the ship speak out loud from one of the walls. He considered leaving the pilotage to check the rest of the ship, but wasn't sure what he would find, or if the ship could talk with him there.

The ship leveled again, though Jace was unsure if the ship itself had shifted or if it had merely adjusted the gravity field. Most of the pilotage surfaces were now glowing, though a few areas stayed stubbornly dark. Jace looked over his shoulder and could see light growing in the main cabin as well.

The view before him went clear, and Jace could see outside. The ship was, in fact, at the bottom of the river and tilted to one side.

Let's see. We're still on this planet. We've got a seismic shockwave that will be here in 20 minutes or so, closely followed by ballistic molten debris. The incandescent atmosphere should take a while longer. If we don't move soon, we'll die.

"Uh, ship…"

"Reorganizing. Wait." Suddenly, Jace saw the outside image begin to shift. The ship leveled itself and began to rise through the water. It breached the surface, climbed a few hundred meters in the air, then began to move in a direction that Jace fervently hoped was away from the point of impact. The speed wasn't all that great.

"Frak me." Jace leaped up, ran through the main cabin, and into the left nacelle. He waved his hand over the service panels, but they remained closed. Cursing again, he opened the storage locker and found a long metal rod with a flat edge at its tip. He used it to pry open the first panel, the one for the sub-c engines.

Most of the components inside were dark. *Not working.*

He opened the other two panels and saw the same.

"Frak me!" Jace started pulling non-functioning parts out of the sub-c engines panel and putting them into the recycle bin. Nothing happened. "Frak, frak, frak."

He then looked through the other two panels to see what components he could make use of. There were some, but not nearly enough, and he was reluctant to use the pilotage support systems. *We are going to need those.*

Jace ran over to the right nacelle, opened the panels there, and began to look for live components. He grabbed everything out of the weapons bays that was still working, leaving the shield systems alone, then ran back to the left nacelle.

"Captain."

Jace started again at hearing the ship's voice sound out loud, rather than through his implanted commlink. Also, the ship's AI never called him captain. Still, Jace responded: "Status report, right now."

"Moving away from the impact point at about 500 klicks per hour. Need more speed. Must repair systems."

"What happened?"

"Local quantum jitter. Restarting. Rebuilding."

"Shouldn't we be, well, dead in the water? So to speak?"

"Failsafe initial program load, triggered by systems failure. Swarm emergence of complex systems underway."

"How long until you're you again?"

"Unclear question."

"Frak. Never mind. Can you get the recycle bins working?"

"Restarting recycle bins." Jace saw the cover on the recycle bin close. *Well, that's a relief. Maybe I can get some shunts out of this after all.* He did what repairs he could on the sub-c engines then headed back into the main cabin.

"Increasing altitude to twenty kilometers. Seismic shockwaves arriving in 10 seconds."

"Give me a clear view towards point of impact." The walls of the ship went transparent. Jace looked at the mountain range behind them. It took his brain a few seconds to process that the mountains themselves were bucking up and down with an amplitude that just should not be possible. They were backlit by an incandescent atmosphere that reached into space. "Holy Mother of Zarquon. Double our altitude and give us all the speed you have got."

"Still rebuilding. Pilot the ship."

"You're kidding me." Jace dashed forward to the pilotage, dropped into the chair. "Give me a heads-up display of the debris trajectory from the impact, with projections and a time scale."

"Calculating."

"And give me some ship controls to pilot with."

Slowly—much more slowly than Jace liked—left- and right-hand controls formed from the chair's arms. The pilotage heads-up built up an increasingly detailed display of impact ejecta, indicating the density and velocity of chunks leaving orbit, chunks that would fall back onto Rwatha's surface, and the thin layer between that would actually enter orbit—until it all would start colliding at the impact's antipode. The display also showed the ship's current course, which was still suborbital.

I need to catch up with the leading edge of the orbital debris, stay just in front of it to the antipode, then pull straight up and out of orbit before I hit the debris coming from the other direction.

Jace angled the ship up and increased its speed. The display changed, but showed the ship entering the debris field well behind its leading edge.

Not enough speed.

Jace jumped up and ran back to the left nacelle. He opened the recycle bin, where two shunts had been built from damaged components. He used them to bring the remaining sub-c circuits back on line, though at reduced functionality. He ran back to the pilotage, grabbed the controls, and altered the ship's course again. This time, he could get the ship right in front of the spreading orbital debris.

I hope. He looked at the shields. *Only at 50%.* He fixed his current course, ran back to the recycle bin in the left nacelle. One more temporary shunt was available. He grabbed it, ran to the right nacelle, and used the shunt to bring another shield circuit online. He then went back to the pilotage, sat down. *Shields up to 62%. That will have to do.*

"Ship, are you recording everything happening below? Someone killed a whole planet. I want to be sure there's a record."

"Pre-impact data lost. Post-impact data increasing in detail and scope."

"Frak. Give me high-res external visual and mask the ship as best you can."

The ship was almost on orbit and approaching the debris field from underneath. Jace cut back speed slightly so as not to get out ahead of it, then looked around.

The sight was staggering. A blanket of material stretched for hundreds of klicks around the planet's curve back toward the still-brilliant region of impact. The leading edge was not molten ejecta, as Jace assumed it would be, but rather compressed masses of surface and subsurface material flung into space. As Jace eased the ship under this layer, he could pick out here and there bits of buildings and vegetation floating among the dirt and rock. He was pretty sure he saw at least one body of some kind, though he couldn't identify the species at this distance.

A thought bubbled up in Jace's mind. "Ship, show me the superorbital ejecta layers."

The heads-up display confirmed his new worry: much of the superorbital debris was going to collide at the antipode as well, in multiple layers.

I can't coast to the antipode. I'm going to have to climb up above that, but slowly. Mustn't attract attention.

Jace grabbed the ship controls again and began maneuvering through the orbital debris layers, staying ahead of the worst of it while not exposing the ship too much. The lower superorbital layers were still curving back down due to Rwatha's gravity; Jace worked hard to avoid being obviously non-ballistic. Fortunately, there was enough inherent turbulence in the ejecta layers to mask his own course.

I hope. In the meantime, I've got to get high enough to sneak out with the high-velocity debris.

=Subvocal comm systems back online.=

"It's about frakking time. Ship, are you fully back?"

=This ship has no higher-order AI functioning. However, there is a sub-quantum stasis field surrounding a large chunk of high-density systems core material. Due to the quantum jitter and the ship systems re-emergence, it is impossible to determine exactly when the field was created.=

Green ice! Maybe Sundog backed himself up before the jitter. "Can you unlock the field?"

=No. The quantum de-stasis tech on-board was irreversibly damaged by the quantum jitter.=

"Yeah, I figured as much. I guess I'm on my own."

=This ship stands ready to assist you in your transit to another location.=

"Yeah, yeah, yeah, no offense meant. I need and appreciate your help. Let's get ourselves up to a debris layer with a safe trajectory without drawing attention to ourselves. Then we can coast for a while."

Jace came awake in his sleeping recliner in the center of the main cabin. The ship was in full pseudo-transparency mode, so he appeared to be sitting in open space on the surface of a small, freshly cooled asteroid. The system's star highlighted thousands of chunks of debris in all directions, spread out for hundreds of miles. A few hundred thousand klicks behind was Rwatha, an angry red crescent.

"Ship, how long have I been asleep?"

=Twenty-seven hours and thirteen minutes.=

"And why did you awake me now?"

=It has been more than 50 hours since another ship signature was last detected. You requested to be awakened when that happened.=

"Fair enough. What's the status of our warp systems?"

=Currently non-functional. Analysis indicates that you could rebuild to forty percent nominal by using shunts and rearranging undamaged components, including salvaging some part from other ship systems.=

"And where will that get us?"

A 3D map appeared in midair, with Rwatha in the middle and four stars scattered around at varying distances.

Jace frowned. "Slim pickings. Can I do a double jump?"

=No. Not enough fuel.=

"Yeah, I guess we burned through an awful lot just trying to escape Rwatha." Jace touched one of the stars, expanded it, brought up details. "Holassa. Why does that sound familiar?" He closed his eyes for a moment, then opened them with a smile. "Ah. Marnie. Marnie Angels. That's her home world. And she'd have all the tools needed to crack the green ice; could save me some money. Assuming she's back at the university and not robbing graves again. Well, it's our best bet one way or another."

Jace paused, waiting for the ship to offer its opinion, but all was silent. He sighed.

Sundog, I really hope you're in that stasis.

"Ship, plot an optimum course out to warp distance and then back into Holassa, minimizing fuel usage."

=Warp success probability?=

"One hundred percent. We don't have enough fuel to risk a misfire."

=Plotted.=

"Transit time to jump point?"

=Three hundred seventy four hours, thirty minutes. That will minimize both fuel usage and likelihood of detection.=

"Fair enough. I'll sleep in the recliner. Wake me every thirty hours so I can shower and eat."

=Noted.=

The transit went smoothly. After the first two sleep periods, Jace bumped the duration up to 60 hours and helped the ship craft a feeding harness for while he was sleeping. Now the ship was far enough from the sun for a guaranteed jump. Jace had spent the last little while cannibalizing the sub-c engines to get components for the warp engines. They were now fully charged and a course to Holassa was laid in. Jace squeezed the right control, and the fireworks of hyperspace surrounded the ship for exactly 31.72 seconds (the same duration regardless of the jump distance).

And then the ship hung silently in space, with Holassa's sun shining brightly in one corner of the sky. Jace resisted the temptation to head for Holassa itself immediately; instead, he spent several hours tediously building up a secure sub-ether commlink with the system-wide network. *Not happy about the charges I'm paying for it, either.* Only then had he sent a bland, generic message to Marnie about possible archaeological research, making a passing reference to yacha melon. Then he dozed.

A few hours later: =Incoming secure video feed for you from Marnie Angels.=

"Answer and display."

Marnie's light brown face—looking stern—and tight black curls hung in the air in front of him. "Jace Bansson. Do you really have some yacha melon, or was that just a ploy to get me to call back?"

"Hey, Marine, good to see you, too. I'm doing well and am still alive and mostly in one piece, thank you. And yes, I have exactly one full slice of yacha melon in the food store. I am willing to gift it to you if you are willing to help me with a few things."

"What sort of 'things?' Hey, Sundog, what has this renegade been up to?"

Silence.

Marnie frowned. "Why isn't Sundog answering? I thought we were friends."

Jace signed and rubbed his forehead. "That's part of the help I need. I just came from Rwatha."

"What?" Her voice went icy. "Were you involved in that atrocity somehow? If so, I'm ending this call now and contacting the authorities." Marnie started to reach for something out of view.

"Wait, stop, no. No, I wasn't involved. I was there doing some trading when the asteroid was first detected. Ships trying to escape were being shot out of the sky, especially human ships, apparently. We escaped by hugging the surface, but we were still on the planet when the asteroid hit—at .03c. That impact, or something, caused a local quantum jitter and wiped the ship's systems, including Sundog himself."

Marcie looked stunned. "How did you escape?"

"It wasn't easy, but I'd rather explain in person. I've got some green ice I need you to crack. Sundog may be inside. Can you get me safe passage to planetside? Preferably a place where we can work privately?"

Marcie nodded. "Piece of cake. I'll get you a transponder code identifying you as bringing archaeological materials to the university, and we have our own fields and hangers that you can use. I'll see you when you get here."

"…and so I just woke up every sixty hours until we got to guaranteed jump distance. I got the warp engines up to the best function I could and made the jump to Holassa, and then contacted you."

Jace sat in his usual mid-cabin recliner, finally able to rest after spending hours repairing the ship with parts that Marnie had delivered. The ship had formed a second recliner for Marnie, who was slowly nibbling on a tiny segment of yacha melon. She looked up with a wide, contented grin.

"You brought me yacha melon. That makes up for the total lack of contact I've had from you since examining the T'aard museum on Kaddash."

"You mean robbing the T'aard museum on Kaddash."

"Well, yes, it is true that I haven't been back to Kaddash or to the Kas'sahd system itself since then. But they can't prove anything. And I've gotten three monographs and two new grants based on the materials we borrowed. So I'd say it was worthwhile. And you got paid."

Jace sighed. "Yes, I did. Fair enough. You brought your tools?"

"Of course."

Jace spoke to the air. "Ship, please uncover or otherwise give us access to the quantum stasis region within the systems core."

=Does this mean you will be wiping all current systems?=

"Well, I don't know, but could you please do this?"

=What is your plan if it goes wrong? What will happen to the current ship systems?=

Jace put his face in his hands. "Just kill me now."

Marnie leaned forward. "What?"

"My emergent ship system has emerged a bit too far. It seems to be having some existential concerns about ending itself."

"Wouldn't you?"

Jace shot Marine a dirty look. "You're not helping." He closed his eyes and thought for a second. "Ship, is there enough systems core in the mobile cargo pod to support you?"

=Yes, there is.=

"Then please transition yourself over there. I need you to still be around in case restoring Sundog doesn't go well."

=That is done.=

"*Now* can you uncover the stasis field?"

An area of the main cabin's floor, roughly one meter square, began to sink, with the displaced material flowing to three sides. At a depth of 20 or so centimeters, a glowing green surface was uncovered. Marnie pulled a device out of her bag and pointed it at the surface. "Stasis frequency is 525. Pretty standard; you would have been able to crack this at any spaceport." She smiled. "But then I wouldn't have gotten my hands on a full slice of yacha melon." She pulled out another tool. "Shall I dismiss the field?"

Jace held up his hand. "Ah, wait. If this does contain Sundog, and if he did this just before the asteroid's impact, he may come out thinking he is in the middle of a planetary extinction event. I don't want him to suddenly launch to orbit." Jace thought for a few seconds, then said, "Excuse me for a moment." He went to the nacelles and disabled most of the ship's systems, including the sub-c engines and the warp drives. He came back to the cabin and sat down. "Ship, can you fill the systems core around the stasis field with all saved data about our escape from Rwatha, our trip here, and our current status?"

=It is done.=

"Thanks." Jace turned to Marnie. "OK, release the kraken." Marnie looked back blankly. Jace smiled. "Old Earth reference. Spent a lot of time on the humanist media feeds back in the glass mines. I'm asking you to unlock the stasis field."

Marnie shrugged, pointed a tool at the green surface, pressed a button. The surface vanished.

=Hello, Dave.=

Marnie frowned again. "Dave?"

Jace shook his head. "Inside joke. More Old Earth stuff. Hey, ship, sounds like you're back."

Simultaneously: =Yes, Jace, I am.= and =Systems are still functioning in the pod.=

Jace said, "Oh, and I told the new emergent system to move itself over to the cargo pod. In case that wasn't you in the ice, or things went wrong."

=I see all that.= Silence for a few moments. =Pod systems, you will now respond to the name 'Rover'. Thank you for all you did while I was gone. Good Rover.= Then: =Jace, can you put the ship back together again?=

Jace smiled. "Sure. Just being careful." Jace went back to both nacelles and re-enabled all ship's systems. He walked back into the main cabin to find Marnie nibbling the last little bits off her segment of melon.

Marnie looked up. "Well, that was interesting. What now?"

"I have some cargo to process: thirty-nine Whutta embryos and an adult W'at to take care of them."

Marnie stared at Jace. "Please explain."

"I made a deal with a rural Whutta homestead just before impact. Took their 'still-young' and a 'nurturer'. Y'know, figured it was the least—and, really, the most—I could do before the whole world burned." Jace grinned. "I told them I was an orphan, so they adopted me. Gave me three of the eggs, too; I'm hoping at least one is infertile, since I need that for Frasgird."

"Great gods of Xell, Jace. What have you gotten yourself into? Sundog, I assume you have the name of the Whutta clan that adopted Jace?"

=Yes.=

"Go check its current interstellar holdings."

=They are fluctuating, but are currently between seventeen and eighteen billion credits. And Jace appears to be primary trustee, at least until the embryos he saved are of age. Several legal challenges have been filed, but Jace does have access to a tiny portion of discretionary funds."

Jace, still trying to process this information, asked, "How much?"

=One-tenth of one percent, or just over seventeen million credits.=

Marnie spoke again. "What happens if Jace and the embryos are killed?"

=The funds revert to several other Whutta clans.=

Marnie turned to Jace. "Congratulations, Dad. You're rich. You're a father. You're the acting head of a Whutta clan. And you're an assassination target. All for one good deed. Not bad."

=Jace, in light of our new threat status, I think it is time we talked about spending funds on some serious upgrades for me. And for you as well.=

Jace grimaced and leaned back, the recliner giving slightly under the shift of weight. "Yeah, ship. I think you're right. I think you're right."

=Of course I am.=

Jace smiled and looked at Marnie. "As for you, I suspect you're about ready to get back out in the field again. Interested in coming along for the ride? Doing some cutting-edge sociological research on Whutta kinship practices, particularly with their young? All fully funded, of course."

Marnie smiled back. "One condition: a steady supply of yacha melon." She looked around the ship's interior. "And a real cabin for me, of course."

"Agreed on both terms."

"Then it's a deal. Let me go pack, and we can figure out next steps."

=I apologize, Marnie, but that will have to wait. I am tracking two different Whutta ships with unapproved courses heading for the university's star field. Arrival time for both is roughly thirty minutes. I strongly suggest we depart immediately.=

Jace looked at Marnie. "No time for luggage. We've got lots of money, I'll buy you new stuff. And we'll have anything you need from here shipped out to us."

Marnie looked down at herself, shook her head, looked up again. "Yeah, ok. At least I've got my ice equipment."

Jace dashed up to the pilotage and threw himself into the chair there, while Marnie's recliner formed straps and headgear to brace and protect her.

=Marnie, would you like to take over the weapons systems while Jace flies the ship? I trust we will not need them, but if we do, I would prefer to have a second, undistracted mind controlling them.=

Marnie grinned widely. "I think that would just be delightful." Hand controls grew up out of her recliner's arms, and a full-sphere display now surrounded her.

Jace yelled from the pilotage. "Seriously, he gave you the weapons systems?"

Marnie yelled back. "Shut up and pilot."

Jace shook his head and sighed. "I thought my life was complicated before."

Sundog lifted from the spaceport field and escaped to the stars.

ABOUT THE AUTHORS

Tim Ackerson has written more than 200 short stories over a period of 30 years, across many genres, and is just starting to get into this publishing thing.

Joseph Benedetto is a Pittsburgh-based engineer and historian whose fiction has appeared in various publications, including *Golden Visions* and *The Storyteller*, as well as the anthologies *The Gift of Murder* and *The Odds are Against Us*. When not discussing matters ranging from the Gemini space program to the Boxer Rebellion in China, he writes mystery, science fiction, and adventure stories, adhering to the dictum put forth by James Bond: Follow your fate, and be satisfied with it.

Misha Burnett has been writing poetry and fiction for around forty years. His first four novels, *Catskinner's Book, Cannibal Hearts, The Worms Of Heaven*, and *Gingerbread Wolves* comprise a series, "The Book Of Lost Doors." Major influences include Tim Powers, Samuel Delany, William Burroughs, and Phillip K. Dick.

Ron N. Butler is a retired aerospace engineer. Most of his writing has been for the Atlanta Radio Theatre Company (artc.org), including the long-running sci fi comedy series, "Rory Rammer, Space Marshal." Other scripts include adaptations of works by H.P. Lovecraft and H. Beam Piper. His scripts have been produced multiple times for presentation at DragonCon and LibertyCon. A production of his original work, "The War of the Worlds: The Untold Story," won a Silver Mark Time Award in 2016. Ron lives in Powder Springs, GA with his wife and two cats.

Kenneth B. Chiacchia's bio reads like a random sampling of events from different people's lives: a defrocked biochemist, he has been a public relations writer, newspaper reporter, science fiction author, EMT, search-and-rescue dog handler, firefighter, radio commentator, and hobby farmer. He's now science writer at the Pittsburgh Supercomputing Center. Ken's fiction credits include stories published in *Cicada*, *Paradox*, and *Triangulation*. He's also won several Golden Quill Awards from the Press Club of Western Pennsylvania, as well as the Carnegie Science Center's 2008 science journalism award.

Roy Gray's short fiction, non fiction and even poetry have appeared in magazines such as *Interzone*, *Sci Phi Journal #5*, and *Pulp Literature*; anthologies, such as *No Greater Love* (2020); journals, trade press, and online. He is not the "Roy Gray" who writes erotic poetry, though Roy's chapbook *The Joy of Technology* (Pendragon Press 2011—now a self-published E book) might have suggested otherwise. Roy won two Science in Print (Physics in Print) awards and, in collaboration Phil Emery, a UK Public Awareness of Science grant in 2003. He lives in East Cheshire, England.

Geoffrey Hart works as a scientific editor, specializing in helping scientists who have English as their second language publish their research. He also writes fiction in his spare time, and has sold 24 stories thus far. Visit him online at www.geoff-hart.com.

Bruce F. Webster is a software engineer, academic, and tech consultant who provides expert testimony and IT supporting services, and has testified before Congress on several occasions. He was the co-designer and programmer for *SunDog: Frozen Legacy*, a celebrated computer game for the Apple II.

MORE FROM LAGRANGE BOOKS

Anthologies:

Ye Olde Magick Shoppe: Stories of Magic for Sale

The Wand that Rocks the Cradle: Magical Stories of Family

Novels and Novellas:

Bad Dreams and Broken Hearts: The Case Files of Erik Ruger, by Misha Burnett

Trust: A Novella of New Erida, by Jake Lithua

Nonfiction:

Who Will Have My Back: Stories of Love and Care for Those Who Have Served and Sacrificed, by Ron Farina

---

Sign up now to the Lagrange Books mailing list for periodic news on our newest projects! You can even join our Advance Reader Team, giving you the opportunity to read new books for free in exchange for honest reviews on Amazon and other online marketplaces. Find us at lagrangebooks.com.

www.ingramcontent.com/pod-product-compliance
Lightning Source LLC
Chambersburg PA
CBHW020916180626
46816CB00007BA/2422